SAVING

For believers of true love and love at first sight.

When Abby Knight's promising start as a family physician is cut short by an abusive relationship, she flees a painful past, trading the hustle and bustle of city living for the more sedate pace of country life.

Her introduction to Peace Springs begins with a freak May snowstorm, a near collision with a moose, a marauding pack of wolves, a mountain man savior, a trek through the snow and spitting llamas.

She's not sure what to think of her choice to join her uncle's family practice in Peace Springs. All in all, it's not a very auspicious beginning.

But leaving her old life, and starting over, is exactly what Abby needs. Meeting Drake, her savior, makes her feel something she hasn't felt in years. Peace. But she's not interested in a new relationship. The only thing she cares about is establishing her medical practice and maybe finding a little bit of peace along the way.

Coming off an abusive relationship makes her wary, but there's no denying the simmering attraction between her and Drake. Only through facing her fears, and living in the moment, will Abby find happiness in the small town of Peace Springs.

But when her past catches up to her, Abby's perfect new life is in jeopardy. Is she strong enough to fight for what she wants and find true love after all?

SAVING ABBY

THE ONE I WANT SERIES

ELLIE MASTERS

JEM PUBLISHING

Editor: Erin Toland

Proofreader: Roxane Leblanc

Published in the United States of America

JEM Publishing

This is a work of fiction. While reference might be made to actual historical events or
existing locations, the names, characters, businesses, places, and incidents are either
the product of the author's imagination or are used fictitiously, and any resemblance
to actual persons, living or dead, business establishments, events, or locales is
entirely coincidental.

* * *

ISBN: 978-1-952625-43-5

DEDICATION

This book is dedicated to my one and only—my amazing and wonderful husband.

Without your care and support, my writing would not have made it this far.

You pushed me when I needed to be pushed.

You supported me when I felt discouraged.

You believed in me when I didn't believe in myself.

If it weren't for you, this book never would have come to life.

ALSO BY ELLIE MASTERS

The LIGHTER SIDE

Ellie Masters is the lighter side of the Jet & Ellie Masters writing duo! You will find Contemporary Romance, Military Romance, Romantic Suspense, Billionaire Romance, and Rock Star Romance in Ellie's Works.

YOU CAN FIND ELLIE'S BOOKS HERE:

ELLIEMASTERS.COM/BOOKS

Military Romance

Guardian Hostage Rescue Specialists

Rescuing Melissa

(Get a FREE copy of Rescuing Melissa

when you join Ellie's Newsletter)

Alpha Team

Rescuing Zoe

Rescuing Moira

Rescuing Eve

Rescuing Lily

Rescuing Jinx

Rescuing Maria

Bravo Team

Rescuing Angie

Rescuing Isabelle

Rescuing Carmen

Military Romance

Guardian Personal Protection Specialists

Sybil's Protector

Lyra's Protector

The One I Want Series

(Small Town, Military Heroes)

By Jet & Ellie Masters

EACH BOOK IN THIS SERIES CAN BE READ AS A STANDALONE AND IS ABOUT A DIFFERENT COUPLE WITH AN HEA.

Saving Ariel

Saving Brie

Saving Cate

Saving Dani

Saving Jen

Saving Abby

Rockstar Romance

The Angel Fire Rock Romance Series

EACH BOOK IN THIS SERIES CAN BE READ AS A STANDALONE AND IS ABOUT A DIFFERENT COUPLE WITH AN HEA. IT IS RECOMMENDED THEY ARE READ IN ORDER.

Ashes to New (prequel)

Heart's Insanity (book 1)

Heart's Desire (book 2)

Heart's Collide (book 3)

Hearts Divided (book 4)

Hearts Entwined (book5)

Forest's FALL (book 6)

Hearts The Last Beat (book7)

Contemporary Romance

Firestorm

(KRISTY BROMBERG'S EVERYDAY HEROES WORLD)

Billionaire Romance

Billionaire Boys Club

Hawke

Richard

Brody

Contemporary Romance

Cocky Captain

(VI KEELAND & PENELOPE WARD'S COCKY HERO WORLD)

Romantic Suspense

EACH BOOK IS A STANDALONE NOVEL.

The Starling

~AND~

Science Fiction

Ellie Masters writing as L.A. Warren

Vendel Rising: a Science Fiction Serialized Novel

TO MY READERS

This book is a work of fiction. It does not exist in the real world and should not be construed as reality. As in most romantic fiction, I've taken liberties. I've compressed the romance into a sliver of time. I've allowed these characters to develop strong bonds of trust over a matter of days.

This does not happen in real life where you, my amazing readers, live. Take more time in your romance and learn who you're giving a piece of your heart to. I urge you to move with caution. Always protect yourself.

1

MOOSE

Nothing helps leave the past behind like a thousand miles and a snowstorm to cover my tracks.

Whoever heard of a blizzard in May?

Isn't there some kind of law against that? It's time for flowers and rain showers, not blinding white and freezing cold. In all the summers I spent in Peace Springs, there's not one memory of snow in May. It feels as if I'm entering a hell that's literally in the process of freezing over.

Not that Peace Springs is hell.

Hell is a thousand miles behind me in Redlands, California. Peace Springs is my future and holds the fondest memories of my life. I spent my summers in the quiet town. I just never saw myself living here as an adult.

I increase the speed of the wipers. Not that it helps. A thick layer of snow builds on the windshield making the road disappear. I flick the high beams, but that only makes things worse. The light reflects off the falling snow, turning the seething mess into an impenetrable wall of white.

On my last check, Peace Springs was less than ten miles away. I'm almost there. Although, it could well be a hundred miles away with the mess outside.

A hot meal, warm bed, and getting off the snowy highway top my list of things to do. I've been on the road since way before dawn, fleeing my past, while leaving sunny California in my dreams.

More like leaving a nightmare behind. My insides clench with lingering fear and righteous anger. Thoughts of Scott make me hyperventilate and that shakiness returns.

I lean forward as if those extra three inches will magically make it easier to see the damn road. As if those three inches will take me further from a painful past.

As for my future, my uncle promises I'll enjoy working in Peace Springs. The idea of being a small-town doc appeals to me, but it intimidates me too.

Do I know enough to help my patients? Are my emergency skills up to par? What will I do when there's no one to look to for help?

I'm fresh out of residency, which means I'm knowledgeable and confident, but also aware of how much I've yet to learn.

The only reason I agreed to this move is because my uncle needs help.

Okay, that's not the only reason.

I desperately needed an excuse to leave Southern California.

My uncle's request came at the best possible time.

Peace Springs is growing, he says. He's looking to retire soon, he says. Taking over his medical practice will be a great experience for a newly licensed family medicine physician. He has more reasons why I should come than I have excuses why I shouldn't.

It makes sense to relocate, for many reasons.

Redlands holds bad memories. My parents' deaths being merely one among many. That's the reason I told him I'd come, but he really gave me the perfect push to finally leave my abusive ex-boyfriend.

A push is exactly what I needed.

A reason to leave.

I wasn't strong enough to leave on my own.

Leaning over the steering wheel, I peer through the windshield and curse the falling snow. For a girl born and raised in Southern California, I'm used to endless sunshine, sprawling cities, tall buildings, and highways six and eight lanes wide. Not this tiny road the locals claim is a highway.

My sigh fills the cab with a mixture of regret and frustration. It also fogs the window. I lean forward, pulling my sleeve over my hand to rub away the moisture.

This is a permanent move, Abby. Embrace it.

I know.

My hopes for establishing a sustainable practice in Redlands died when one punch to my face became one too many.

I glance at the back seat to check on the Boston fern. The houseplant is the only thing Scott let me take. He thinks I'm throwing a hissy fit and will come crawling back to him. That I'm testing him.

But I'm not.

I took the fern, and by hell or high water, I'll transport the darn thing all the way up the coast. Not because the plant means anything to me, but because Scott wouldn't let me take anything else.

My entire life is condensed into three suitcases, a potted plant, and ... Holy crap!

A moose!

My scream shatters the silence. Stomping on the brakes, I wrench the steering wheel hard to the right.

The massive animal stands placidly in the middle of the road—watching me—breathing out—whereas my pulse thunders in my ears and my stomach leaps to my throat.

The tires slide over the ice. Counter-steering, I point the car back in the direction I want to go. I've read that's what you're supposed to do, but it doesn't work. My Jeep slides into a spin.

Coming full circle, the moose and I trade stares again. It snorts, blowing out twin plumes of steam from its nostrils, while the Jeep launches off the road.

I plow straight into a ditch.

A loud bang sounds. Something slams into my face. A fine, white powder coats the inside of the car, making me cough and gasp for air.

The airbag deployed, saving my life, but damn does it hurt. My heart hammers and the ragged pull of my breaths scrapes in my ears.

"No, no, no!"

This can't be happening.

And what's up with moose on the loose?

What's next? Lions, tigers, and bears?

More likely, I'll find mountain lions, wolves, and bears.

Outside, snow piles up on the hood of my car.

I punch the airbag out of the way. The bridge of my nose hurts. My cheekbones are tender. My eyes sting. My lids drag against the grit from the powder. I go into damage control.

Okay, what hurts?

No pain in my ribs. My shoulder hurts from the seatbelt, but nothing seems to be broken. I wiggle my toes and move my legs.

No pain there.

Where's my phone? It was in the drink holder a second ago.

I search while the outside temperature steals my precious heat. Staying put might seem wise, but what if no help ever comes?

There hasn't been another vehicle on the road for miles. Even in the daylight, will anyone see my Jeep? Or will the snow cover it, encasing me in a chilly grave?

I flip on the emergency flashers.

My phone?

There, on the passenger floorboard. I grab it and stab at the screen.

No reception.

Not that it matters. The battery is down to less than five percent and won't last much longer.

The engine sputters, coughs, and dies. The heater quits. A chill creeps in through the windows. I place my palm against the glass and withdraw with a hiss. There are only a few hours left until midnight, which means it will only get colder outside.

Thanks to that damned moose, I'm half-buried in a ditch. Real fear sets in as the encroaching cold seeps through the metal of my car.

There's no way to get my Jeep out of the ditch. I try to crank the engine over, but nothing happens.

Do I wait out the storm? If I get the engine running, is it safe to keep it going? I remember something about keeping the exhaust clear, but with less than a quarter tank of gas, the engine won't last through morning.

Staying warm and dry is my top priority.

And finding help.

Twice, I turn the key, but the engine refuses to start. Do I stay with the vehicle? Or will I be safer walking along the road?

The wind dies down. A stillness hangs over the countryside. It's oddly tranquil as the snow continues to fall.

If it wasn't for my life and death situation, I might take a moment to admire the beauty of it all, but there's no time for that.

First objective - stay warm.

Well, walking will generate body heat. Sitting in the car won't.

A glance back at the jumble of my luggage and I make a decision.

I have a thin coat, a hat, plenty of shirts, and even a pair of sweats. Layers will be the key.

"Sorry, Boston, you're on your own." That poor fern doesn't stand a chance.

I lost you too soon.

I feel bad about leaving the fern behind, but what am I going to do? Tuck it under my arm? Carry it in the crook of my elbow? It shouldn't mean as much to me as it does—it's a plant—but I need that poor fern to survive.

After many contortions inside the vehicle, I'm out of breath but warmer. I layered on seven shirts and shoved my legs into a pair of sweats, tugging them over my jeans. I don't have anything but sneakers and sandals in my luggage.

Hello, California girl here!

A good pair of boots would be nice.

One last look outside makes me weigh the pros and cons of leaving my Jeep. Once I step outside, there's no telling how deep the drifts might be. Cold feet will make walking difficult. But cold, wet feet will make my trek downright treacherous.

Not to mention the very real and present danger of frostbite.

Shit, I don't have the experience for this.

Turning back to my luggage, I grab three sets of socks, just in case the pair I have on gets wet during my climb out of the ditch. I grab another pair to put over my hands in place of gloves.

Time to go.

I give a silent prayer, hoping someone happens to be cruising the highway.

I shove and then kick the door to get it open. Once I get the door open wide enough, I slip out and promptly sink to my knees.

Frigid air bites my nose. My cheeks prickle with the cold. Snow encases my feet, freezing my ankles.

I'm so screwed.

"Nice way to extend the welcome mat, Montana." I spit at the wind, cursing my current predicament.

A gust of wind blows snow into my eyes, making them water.

Time to get out of this ditch.

On my climb out, I stumble and fall face-first into the snow more than once. The tip of my nose burns with the cold. My cheeks sting until I can't feel them anymore. My fingers go numb. Deep shivers rack my body.

I finally make it to the road and already question my sanity about leaving the vehicle. However, the Jeep will be my coffin if I stay.

It's this, or nothing.

As I feared, the Jeep is completely hidden from view. No chance anyone will spot it. The snow completely encases the hazard lights and obliterates any sign of my skid.

Where the hell is that damn moose? If I die because I tried to save its life, there is going to be hell to pay.

I wrap my arms around myself to conserve body heat. My sneakers are damp, but I can't do anything about that. Other than my rapid breathing, the night is almost tranquil. The snow sizzles as it falls, which feels all kinds of peaceful.

Except my survival is at stake.

Getting back to my feet, I stamp away the cold, urging circulation back into my frozen toes. At least there's one positive in all this mess. I know which way to go, if not how far I have to hike.

Less than ten miles for certain.

Probably fewer than five.

I can do this.

As long as I keep to the road, and keep moving, I should reach Peace Springs within the hour.

Two at most.

Turning left, I take my first step. Head down, I turn into the wind and walk toward Peace Springs.

About an hour later, the wind kicks up. Each step becomes a chore. All I want to do is stop, curl up, and sleep. Not once do I see headlights. Nor do I see lights from farms or ranches on either side of the road. Open sky territory, there's no sign of humanity.

That never happens in California.

Time drags. My molars knock against one another. The muscles of my jaw bunch with the constant chattering of my teeth. And my back—the small of my back tightens with each windy gust.

This is hell, but I don't stop. I take another step, and then one more. My thoughts drift with the swirling snow, thinking back to another time. A situation I barely escaped. Hopefully, my poor choices, and Scott, will stay in my past.

A crackling of branches sounds to my left.

Did the moose return?

I wish I had a flashlight. Instead, I move to the center of the road.

More breaking branches; an animal smaller than a moose from the sound of it.

Like I'm some expert.

Okay then. Dog or coyote?

Dogs are friendly and not a threat. Coyotes tend to be skittish and scared of humans. As long as whatever's moving in the brush isn't a wolf, I'm happy to let it be.

Silence follows, and I breathe out, teasing myself for every flinch I make in response to the random noises of nature. Every little sound seems amplified, and that makes me jumpy.

An ear-piercing howl breaks the stillness. A deep wailing. It carries through the air and crashes against my ears, making my pulse race.

I come to a halt, heart jackhammering in my chest.

A streak of red flashes in front of me, less than ten feet away. I jump but force myself to calm down. That animal is too small to be a wolf.

Fox, maybe?

I try to laugh, but it comes out strangled and scared.

The squeaking of snow sounds behind me, followed by a low huff.

I spin and come face-to-face with a pack of timber wolves. The lead animal points its nose to the sky and lets loose a long, piercing howl.

The skin-crawling noise splits the night air. The wolf paws the ground, snorts, and faces me down. It raises thin lips and gives a throaty growl while the other wolves hunker down and snarl.

2

WOLVES

THE SNARL OF THE PACK ALPHA FREEZES ME IN MY TRACKS. THE WOLF stands waist—no—chest high. Massive. When did wolves get so big?

And their teeth?

Sharp and menacing, I take a step back.

The moist air from its exhaled breath coalesces into a fog, which coils around its muzzle. Its upper lip pulls back into a snarl.

It looks hungry.

Very hungry.

"Don't move." A deep voice calls out somewhere behind and to the right of me.

The alpha wolf shakes its massive head. Its head cocks to the side, ears rotating to locate the source of that voice. It sniffs the air but doesn't seem to be able to lock onto a scent.

It growls again, lifting the hairs on my nape. I'm moments from doing exactly the opposite of what that voice commands.

Don't move? Is he crazy?

All that wolf has to do is launch at me and I'm toast. Its paws will land on my shoulders. Its weight will push me down. Those snarling teeth will snap and clamp around my throat.

The others in the pack support their alpha, forming a loose semicircle behind it. Their strategy's clear and terrifying. Each animal can attack without getting in the others' way.

Talk about coordinating a kill.

"Don't make any sudden moves." The man behind me is so damn calm. "Run, and you're dead."

No shit, Sherlock.

A wolf toward the back of the pack pricks up its ears, rotating them toward the man's voice. It scents the air, nostrils flaring. The wolf looks to its leader, head swiveling with indecision.

My hands tremble and my breath catches. An hour ago, my biggest concern was hitting a moose. Now, I face a pack of wolves.

"What do I do?" My voice cracks.

"Take a slow step back."

Technically, that's moving. Exactly what he told me *not* to do.

I maintain eye contact with the lead wolf while I slide my right foot back. The animal lowers its head, lips curled. The wolf growls as if daring me to run. Instinct tells me that'll be the cue that initiates the wolf's attack.

"That's it," the unidentified man says. "Take another step back."

The rear wolf's ears twitch, rotating to locate the voice. It gives a low whine and dips its head to huff at the snow.

I transfer my weight to my right foot and slide the left one back. The alpha hunkers down, nose brushing the snow. It takes a slow step forward.

"Again," the man urges. "I need more space for my shot."

I snap my head around. "Your shot?"

My sudden movement triggers the wolf.

The alpha leaps.

A shot rings out.

I scream.

A painful yelp sounds, and then the alpha lands in a heap at my feet with a whimper. Its forepaws scrabble at the air.

A blur of tawny gray springs from my left. Another shot rings out, followed by a pained yelp and another hard landing.

"I told you not to move!"

I cast around, searching for the man, but find nothing. At my feet, the alpha whimpers. Its forepaws scrabble at the snow until it takes a final, shuddering breath.

The three remaining wolves look uncertain; their cohesion destroyed. I think they'll make a run for it.

Couldn't be more wrong.

The wolves attack.

I stumble back beneath an onslaught of fur, teeth, and claws. More gunshots split the air. Wolves cry out, whimper, and fall dead at my feet.

"You killed them!" I scream. "Why did you kill them?"

Where the hell is he? And why can't I see him?

I peer into a landscape of white on white and see nothing recognizable.

"To save your life," he says. "What the hell are you doing out here anyway?" Dressed in shades of white and gray, I barely pick out the man's form from the background.

He's massive.

Tall and broad-shouldered, his winter gear protects him from the cold. The tops of his gloves are pulled back, freeing his fingers which grip the deadly rifle.

I tuck my hands under my armpits seeking warmth. My fingertips tingle with the cold and what I hope isn't the beginning of frostbite. The thin cotton of my socks provides little protection from the plunging temperatures.

A hood casts his face in shadow. White and gray fabric covers most of his face. Beneath the hood, a pair of thick goggles hide his eyes.

Heavy boots encase his feet. Mid-calf, fabric gathers halfway above and below his boots. I've seen those before. Called gaiters, they're designed to wrap around the shins and cover the opening between a person's pants and their shoes.

They keep snow out of boots.

Wish I had some of those.

"Did you have to kill them?"

He wiped out the entire pack. I loathe guns and hate violence of any sort, especially against animals, but if he hadn't been here ... I'm not going to think about what might have happened.

"Those vermin are a menace, not to mention what would've happened to you."

"Vermin? They're endangered. You took out the whole pack."

"Were."

"Huh?"

"Were endangered. Now, they're a menace. The fact they were stalking you should be telling enough."

He climbs the last few feet up the bank and approaches me. His long stride devours the distance between us. Cocking his head, he regards me for a long moment. His goggles glitter with the ambient glow of the snow all around us.

While I can't see his eyes, his gaze falls on me, taking in the trembling of my hands, the shaking of my shoulders, and my general distress. The corners of his lips twitch. I can't say if it's from irritation or something else.

"What are you doing out here dressed like that?" He makes a vague gesture, sweeping from my head to my toes. His voice, deep and rumbly, is strangely seductive. It curls around me, twining around my body, settling in deep, where it does strange things to my insides.

He gives zero reaction he's aware of the effect he has on me. Which is for the best.

I wrap my arms around myself, trying to preserve precious body heat, as his stare lingers longer than socially acceptable. I stiffen my spine and roll my shoulders back.

"You think I'm out here by choice? I crashed my Jeep; ran into a ditch. I'm not out for a midnight stroll." I roll my eyes. "This is the best I had."

He places the butt of his rifle on the toe of his boot, and a low, throaty chuckle spreads from his chest, bursting forth into a deep, belly laugh.

"There's nothing funny about this."

"How many layers are you wearing?" He's looking at me again. Scrap that; he's peeling away the layers with the heat of his gaze. A gaze I can't see because of his goggles.

"Why are you laughing at me?" I step back from the dead wolves, eager to place distance between me and the bodies. "You should've given a warning shot and run the wolves off."

In death, the animals appear majestic. Peaceful. They don't look nearly as ferocious as they did a few minutes ago.

"Warning shot? Why would I do that?"

"To scare them away. They would've run. You didn't have to kill them."

"What part of vermin do you not understand?" His frosty reply makes it sound like I'm an idiot.

My back bristles beneath the challenge. I don't like anybody questioning my intelligence.

"They're an endangered species." My fingers curl in frustration within my makeshift gloves. The thin cotton of my socks does little to block the wind. Now that I'm standing still, the cold renews its attack, seeping through the thin cotton protecting my skin.

"You're wrong. Wolves are vermin, breeding like there's no tomorrow. I saved your life and you're worried about killing a few wolves?" He sounds genuinely incredulous.

One thing is obvious. He's not happy I'm out here alone. Hell, I'm not happy being out here alone. This is not how I saw my return to Peace Springs going.

I know little about the debate surrounding wolf preservation efforts, except there are two sides to the story. Man nearly brought timber wolves to the edge of extinction, and reintroduction efforts are a topic for debate.

"I don't see how that gives you license to kill them when you could've run them off." I fist my hands and place them on my hips.

He laughs. "Obviously, you know nothing about wolves." He grabs a wolf body and drags it to the side of the road. "This pack has been harrying the sheep and cattle all through winter. They've even taken out a few of Bert's llamas."

Llamas?

This is cattle country. Surely, he means cattle? Or maybe, I'm hearing things.

"It still doesn't give you the right to kill them." I stand my ground, not giving an inch as far as my argument goes.

He fixes me with a penetrating stare. It doesn't look like the cold bothers him at all, whereas my core body temperature is dropping to dangerous levels. I tuck my hands under my armpits.

"For the record, Fish, Wildlife, and Parks gives me the right to kill these wolves. I can kill up to a hundred if I want."

"A hundred?"

"Don't sound that endangered anymore. What part of menace do you not understand? And you're welcome, by the way."

"Welcome, for what?"

"For saving your life."

I hate that he's right, but damn his arrogance. For that reason alone, I don't say thank you.

My father used to say I'm too stubborn for my own good. But that stubborn streak is the one thing that gave me the tenacity to finish medical school and complete my residency, despite everything that happened.

I take in a deep breath and blow it out. "Can you tell me how much farther it is to Peace Springs?"

He points back the way I came. "About eight miles that way."

My jaw drops. "Excuse me?"

"Eight miles." He slings his rifle over his shoulder and drags another wolf body off the road. "Now, care to tell me why you're headed out of town, dressed like that in the middle of a snowstorm?"

My coat isn't meant for winter weather. I bought it on a whim because I liked the color. Right now, seven layers of cotton shirts, jeans covered by sweats, and a lightweight coat have me wishing for something more like what the man is wearing.

"I told you, my Jeep ran off the side of the road. I thought it was this way."

"It?"

"Peace Springs."

"Lady, you're really mixed up." He pulls another two wolves off the highway.

Tears of frustration brim in my eyes. I wipe at my cheeks. In the last hour or two, I've probably covered three or four miles. There's no way I'll make it eight more.

"Listen, I'd really appreciate some help."

"Looks like you need it." He comes for the last animal and pulls it over to join the others.

The man towers over me, having at least a foot, maybe a foot and a half, in height over me. The top of my head barely comes to his shoulders. His arrogance makes me want to stamp my foot. It's bad enough I have to ask, but for him to rub it in? That's cold.

"Why are you out here?" Despite my anger, I'm curious.

"Told you." His velvety voice washes over me, twisting my insides in the good kind of way. Sultry. Seductive. He's impressive. "I was tracking that pack. Why else would anyone be out in this godforsaken weather?" He steps toward me, concern replacing the snide comments from earlier. "How long have you been out?"

"An hour, maybe two? I thought I'd be able to walk to town."

"In this?"

"The snow stopped falling after my accident."

"You should have stayed with your car. You're going to freeze to death out here. What were you thinking getting out and walking in this?" Finally, he shows some compassion.

I don't answer him. The longer I stand in one place, the colder I get, and I can't stop my teeth from chattering.

He glances at my feet and makes a *tsking* noise. "You're not going to last much longer." With a rasp, he lowers the zipper of his coat and shrugs out of the thick material.

"Honey, put this on before you freeze to death. We have a long walk ahead of us."

"How far is your car?" I ask with a shudder.

"Car? Don't you pay attention? I was hunting that pack. My truck is back at Bert's." He points across the field. "We're going overland."

A creeping sense of dread shoots down my spine, making me quake, not from the cold, but from fear.

"Overland?" There's no way I'm leaving the road.

He tilts his head, looking at my feet with those weird goggles. "There's no way you're making it in sneakers." Gripping his chin, he seems deep in thought.

I take the opportunity to wrap myself in his jacket. A deep woodsy scent fills my nostrils and has me taking a deep breath. The faint aroma of male sweat, sultry and dark, smells divine. I tug at the collar and pull it close. Shamelessly, I take another inhale. His chuckle brings my head snapping up.

"It works better when you zip it, not sniff it."

Getting caught smelling his jacket, searing heat fills my cheeks. No man deserves to smell that good. Thankfully, he turns his attention to my feet, which gives me one last opportunity to take in his dark and sultry scent.

"We need to do something about your feet and the snow." Bending down, he unfastens the white gaiters over his boots.

"I can't take those." I hold out a hand, palm up, in refusal.

"You're taking them. Impossible to hike cross-country in sneakers, and I'm not carrying you."

Instead of handing me the gaiters and making me figure out how to secure them around my calves, he kneels and taps the top of his thigh.

"Put your foot here, and we'll see what we can do."

A little hesitant, I don't argue. Especially when this stranger is going out of his way to not only give me, literally, the coat off his back, but his gaiters as well. He snaps the top and bottom buttons then tacks down the Velcro strip binding the whole thing together. He proceeds to pull an elastic tab over the back of my heel and settles it against the sole of my shoe.

"Try not to drag your feet, or the strap will slip off. These should keep most of the snow out of your shoes."

When I put my foot down and test the elastic strap, he stands. His size intimidates me, and I can't help but take an involuntary step back. I'm what I call *tall enough for my feet to reach the ground*, which means I'm short and more than a little self-conscious about my five-foot-three frame.

Standing so close, I crane my neck to see his face, or what little there is to see. He hasn't removed the goggles or the fabric covering his nose, mouth, and chin. But the real reason I step back is because of the strange thing being so close to him does to my insides.

Needle-thin flakes fill the air, more snow coming down. I zip the jacket, not because he told me to, but because I want to keep the residue of his warmth, and maybe some of his scent, inside the jacket.

"Shouldn't we call someone?"

The road still looks far better than a hike cross-country. I swallow the lump of fear rising in my throat.

The deep rumble of his voice rolls back toward me. "Cell reception sucks this far from town. Don't worry, it's a short hike to Bert's."

He heads off the road, waving for me to follow. Leaving the safety of the road goes against my better judgment, but he knows two things I don't.

First, he knows where we need to go. Left to my own devices, I would have hiked into the wilderness and froze to death or run into another pack of wolves.

Second, I follow for another, more unsettling reason. This man knows what he's doing. His confidence fills me with a sense that everything will be all right.

"How far?"

"Two miles." Behind us, another piercing howl fills the night sky. The man stops and turns around. "Damn wolves. Come on, let's get a move on."

3

LLAMAS

TWO MILES, HE SAYS. JUST A LITTLE FURTHER, HE SAYS. IT FEELS LIKE we've been hiking for ten miles instead of two. My feet are lead bricks. Every step is a massive investment of energy.

I want to curl up into a ball and just—stop.

But the man who shot the wolves sets a relentless pace.

We hike cross-country for well over an hour, and nothing but rolling white stretches out in front of us. The sky is a featureless gray. Backlit by the moon, the clouds glow with a faint, ethereal light, providing barely enough illumination to show the way.

Which way that might be, I have no idea.

Snow drifts downward, piling up beneath my feet. We aren't back in blizzard-like conditions, but this overland travel is challenging.

And, I'm hot!

Sweat slicks down my back. It drips between my breasts. Perspiration saturates the band of my bra and chafes my skin.

As thankful as I am for the coat, I unzip it and let it flap in the gusting wind. I'd take the damn coat off, except my guide would disapprove.

Despite the fact my body is a toaster oven, the same cannot be said of my face. The frigid temperatures prick at my cheeks and numb the tip of my nose. I rub my nose repeatedly, even hold my hands in front of my face like a shield, trying to warm the tender tip.

And my ears!

They burned like fire when the flurries kicked. Now, I can't feel my ears at all.

Which is bad.

Very bad.

I fall back on my wilderness medicine courses in residency and medical school, pulling up everything I know about exposure to extreme cold.

Numbness means the skin and cartilage of my ears is frozen or in the process of freezing. My medical mind dredges up facts differentiating frostnip from frostbite.

If I hold my hands over my ears, my nose burns. If I hold my hands over my nose, my ears burn. In deciding which disfigurement I'd rather live with, it's hard to decide. I settle on keeping my nose and sacrificing my ears. At least I can cover those with a hat.

Lifting the hood of his coat helps somewhat to restore circulation to my numb ears. Blood rushes in, bringing warmth to the nearly frozen tissue with a fiery burn of sensation. But the hood traps in my body heat as well, making me sweat even more.

I was cold while walking on the road. My movement was barely enough to keep my body temperature from plunging to dangerous levels. Now, I'm wishing for an air conditioner.

And whoever my savior is, his powerful legs devour the ground. I spend the first ten-minutes jog-stepping to keep pace. Finally, I decide he needs to match my pace, not the other way around.

We cross a pasture, and it takes a few minutes before he realizes how far behind I fall. I struggle through a knee-high drifting of snow while he waits, saying nothing.

His brooding silence irritates me, but I'm content to not engage in unnecessary conversation.

The moment I catch up, I expect a short reprieve. That doesn't happen. He continues his trek, slowing down out of consideration for my much shorter stride, but never stopping for a break. I curse him silently behind his back.

The gaiters are amazing. Despite plunging mid-calf, and in some cases, up to my knees in snow, the waterproof fabric keeps my lower legs free from snow and prevents it from sneaking into my shoes. Nevertheless, snow cakes the top of my sneakers and melts through. My feet are wet, cold, and numb. They feel ten pounds too heavy, and I struggle with every step.

Several times, I ask how much farther. His response, *"Just a little more,"* turns sour after my fifth or sixth demand.

We hike in silence, broken only by the crunching of our shoes over virgin snow and the occasional gusting of the wind. After that first keening wail, we hear nothing else from that distant wolf pack.

And then, it happens.

When I lose all hope of ever making it to anything resembling civilization, he crests a steep rise and stops.

I climb after him, slipping more times than not, wondering why he doesn't offer his hand. At the top of the hill, I see a miracle.

A tiny house sits in the valley below. Light spills out of its windows to splash onto the virgin snow, promising warmth inside. I clasp my hands and bring them to my mouth. A few hundred yards and I can strip out of all these layers, and maybe, just maybe, I'll be warm again.

He points down the slope to a barbed-wire fence.

"We have to crawl over the wire. I would've taken us to the gate, but that's not for another mile to the west. Be careful, and don't snag yourself on the barbs. It'll leave a scar, and you'll need a tetanus shot."

I know all about painful tetanus shots. Not that I need to worry. All my immunizations are up to date. Besides, the barbs have to penetrate seven, no eight, layers of fabric before piercing my skin.

"And we'll have to be careful crossing the field," he continues. "I don't think the llamas are out. Bert keeps them in the barn in weather like this."

I expect sheep or cattle, but llamas? Livestock scares the crap out of me. Cows are placid creatures, but I don't trust something that weighs close to a ton. Sheep are basically overstuffed dogs. They're stupid as shit, and didn't I read somewhere that they bite? Maybe that was about llamas.

As for llamas, I know nothing about them except they're the dorkiest animals I've ever seen.

"Um, okay?"

His chuckle fills the stillness. I have yet to see his face and imagine him any number of ways.

What does he look like?

Tall and handsome?

Or tall and fearsome?

Unlike me, he isn't out of breath and looks like he could continue this pace all day long. He's definitely comfortable outdoors. I'm dying, overexerted and huffing every breath. He looks like he's out for an afternoon stroll.

I wish I could see his eyes.

We move across the field, scanning left and right. He keeps those odd goggles on the entire time, hiding his face and making it impossible to read his expressions. Other than the deep timbre of his voice, and his powerful frame, he remains a complete mystery.

"Llamas?" I ask.

Who is Bert, and why does he have llamas? My wilderness guide and savior speaks about Bert as if I should know him.

I'm used to horses, cattle, and sheep. Llamas are unexpected. Next thing my guide is going to tell me, there's an ostrich farm nearby.

He speaks over his shoulder, leading the way down the hill. "Well, they aren't like horses or cattle, that's for sure."

"Why's that?"

"You really aren't from around here, are you?" His voice echoes into the breach of wintery silence. All around us, the land slumbers, caressed to quiet by the rumble of his voice.

What does he look like under that mask and beneath those goggles? The mystery is killing me.

"City girl?" His voice holds a little more than a bit of scorn.

"I'm not from the city, but definitely not the country."

"Suburbs then," he says with distaste.

"Not sure Redlands is considered the suburbs. More like a little, big town." I don't want to continue that conversation, not when his tone is so disparaging. "Tell me about these llamas."

He huffs another laugh. "They're curious and alert creatures— related to camels, which means they spit. I'd keep your distance."

"Well, I think I'm capable of staying out of range of llama spit."

"Maybe," he says. "Their necks are longer than you think. You've been warned."

"I'll stay back."

"Well, if any of them are out, I'd suggest getting behind me."

"Why?"

"This herd has been harried by the wolves. They're a bit strung out. They're likely to attack a stranger."

Great. Don't impale myself on the barbed wire. Avoid spitting llamas and don't get trampled by one either.

"Anything else I need to know?"

"Nope."

I can't see his face but imagine a smile behind the mask. He's probably having a good laugh at the poor *city girl*. Well, I can handle anything country thrown my way.

"Well, lead on," I say, gesturing toward the house across the field. "I can't wait to see my first llama."

"Definitely a city girl," he says with a rumble of his deliciously deep voice.

"You say that like it's a bad thing." My words come out more defensive than I intend. My savior is light on the compliments, inclined to point out every mistake I make.

Not that it was my choice to nearly run down a moose.

Or walk the wrong way, headed out of town instead of toward. Okay, that may have been a colossal mistake, but I swear I was headed the right way.

We reach the bottom of the hill and approach a snarl of barbed wire fencing. I'm not clear on how he expects me to make it over the fence.

He places the sole of his boot on the lowest strand and steps down. The action opens a six-inch gap. Not something I'm able to crawl through. I give him a dubious look.

He gestures toward me. "Come here."

I cross my arms and stay where I am. "Maybe we should find this gate?"

"You don't have another mile in you, city girl. Now take my coat off and give it here."

While I may have been complaining about being overly warm a few minutes ago, standing at the base of the hill finds me shivering again. I don't want to give up the coat, but his command doesn't allow for argument.

I shrug out of the coat and hand it over. Right then, a gust blows the snow into a flurry, making me shiver. He wraps his coat around the upper strands of wire, forming a U-shape. Then he lifts. The six-inch gap widens.

"Hurry up," he says. "This is harder than it looks."

I rush forward, eyeing the opening, hoping his arm doesn't give out while I'm halfway through. One glance at the fullness of muscles bunched under his shirt, and I don't have much to worry about.

Picking my way over the exposed wire, I clear the fence.

He releases his hold, and the gap in the fence collapses, leaving him on the outside of the fencing.

"How are you ..."

I don't get to finish my sentence because he places his hand on the nearest post and vaults over the wire like it's nothing.

Damn.

He twists around and lands beside me while I unabashedly stare, admiring his strength and agility. He frees the coat from a barb with a little rip of fabric. Great, now I have to buy him a new coat.

"Come on," he says. "Almost there. Put the coat back on."

"I'm a little overheated," I say.

"Don't care," he says, shoving the coat at me. "It doesn't take long to freeze out here, and we're not inside yet. Put the coat on."

His insistent tone leaves no room for argument. I take the coat and slip it on. I've been taught to be cautious. Not to trust. Yet here I'm, following a stranger into a house in the middle of nowhere.

It doesn't help it is nearly midnight.

Past midnight? I don't know what time it is. He could do anything to me, and no one would ever know. Maybe it would've been better to stay with my Jeep?

It doesn't take long before he's ahead of me again, marching toward the inviting ranch-style home.

A single-story structure, it has a classic, rambling farm feel to it, but what draws my eye, and energizes my step, is the thin trail of smoke twisting up from the chimney. I'd give my firstborn to sit in front of that fire right about now.

My savior picks up his pace. The distance between us grows. Remembering what he said about testy llamas, I stumble to a jog, intent on closing the gap. Or maybe, I just really want to be out of this damn weather.

Fresh wood smoke fills my nostrils: a thick, homey scent. My savior waits at a wooden gate, holding it open. I step past him and take a deep breath. The ordeal of my evening is almost over.

I'm safe.

He latches the fence and walks beside me the remaining distance. His impressive height dwarfs my much smaller frame, but something about it feels strangely natural.

This feels like a Hallmark moment, as if I'm finally coming home. I place my hand on my savior's arm and feel him tense. Ignoring his reaction, I let my words spill.

"When I forget to tell you later how grateful I am for your help tonight, please know that I am."

The tension in his body evaporates and he places his arm around my shoulder. It's the first real physical contact between us other than when he fastened the gaiters around my legs. Tugging me close, he gives my shoulder a squeeze.

"City girl, the people of Peace Springs look out for one another. No need to say thank you, but you're welcome. Now, let's get you inside."

With a tug, he pulls at the strap of the odd goggles and yanks off his hat, revealing midnight black hair and the darkest, coal-black eyes I've ever seen. A jagged scar stretches from the corner of his mouth all the way up to his eye.

I gasp and take a step back. Normally a disfigurement like that would mar a person's beauty, but it does exactly the opposite with him.

Ruggedly handsome isn't sufficient to describe his aching beauty. Even the ferociousness of his expression speaks to a great pain in his past. Scar aside, it's the black depths of his eyes that hint at something dangerously intoxicating.

The intensity of his expression pins me in place; perhaps he waits to see my reaction to his disfigurement. I can't help but reach out. I try to trace the contours of his majestic face, my frozen fingers tremble, but he grabs my wrist, yanking it away.

"What the hell do you think you're doing?" Lightning quick, he eliminates the distance between us, forcing me to take a step back. Only, his grip tightens, dragging a strangled cry from my throat. He pulls me close, close enough for the heat of his breath to warm my cheeks.

He crowds my space. Steals my air. Heats my skin, and hell if the strangest thoughts don't rush through my head. Eye level with his chest, he towers over me. While no part of him, except for his hand, touches me, it feels as he's everywhere at once.

My entire body takes notice, but instead of recoiling—something I would do if this was Scott—I lean in.

"Get a good hard look at it, city girl. Take your fill, but don't ever assume you can touch me like that again. I'm not some circus freak you can gawk at."

My breaths stagger and lurch, confused, but then his words sink in. I struggle to fill my lungs and respond to his angry words.

"I didn't—I'm not ..."

His scar is a thing of beauty. There's not one thing repulsive about it, but I don't get to tell him that.

"Hey." A gravelly voice calls out. Light spills from an open doorway onto the expanse of untouched snow. "Drake? Is that you?" The man gives a low whistle. "Whatcha got there?"

Drake releases my wrist, practically tossing me aside. "Found that pack and picked up a straggler."

"I'm not a straggler." I stomp my foot, frustrated with how things are turning out.

"Bert will take care of you, city girl." Drake practically shoves me toward the man, who I assume is Bert.

"Name's Bert Winston. Nice to meet you." He stretches out his hand to take mine. His eyes twinkle in the faded moonlight, then shift with concern toward my savior, Drake. Bert's brow arches in question. "And who might you be?"

"Hi, my name's Abby."

4

WHISKEY

PERHAPS IT'S NOT FAIR TO STEREOTYPE THE LLAMA RANCHER, BUT WHEN Drake mentioned llamas and Bert, I imagined a hick in baggy suspenders, worn-out jeans, a plaid shirt, and cowboy boots. I even included a piece of straw sticking out between the gap I imagined between his two front teeth having. Oh, and a cowboy hat.

Bert is none of that.

He surprises me in his wool trousers, buttoned-up Oxford, tweed blazer, sleek boots, and what looks like a fedora perched with impeccable flair atop his head.

Meticulously groomed, even his gray beard is trimmed and combed. Instead of chewing on a piece of straw, Bert puffs a cigar. Deep laugh lines crinkle the skin around his eyes, which tells me the most important thing about this man. That huge smile of his is a comfortable, lifelong, friend.

I adore him on sight.

He feels familiar, like coming home, as if whatever ails me will disappear the moment I step foot across his doorstep. He's kind, welcoming, warm, and—peaceful.

I've never felt anything like this before.

Blueish-black smoke floats upward from the tip of the cigar to curl around his head. A puff makes the tip of the cigar glow. He even blows honest to goodness smoke rings. And what's that in his hand?

I lean forward, eyes pinching, and catch the unmistakable title of the book. A *Wuthering Heights* fan?

No way.

I label him a fan without feeling guilty about it because the edges of the leather-bound cover are worn and the pages curl as if it has been lovingly handled many wonderful times.

I look into his twinkling eyes, such a contrast to Drake's black pools of mystery and pain. Jade-colored gems round with mirth as Bert puffs on his cigar.

"Well, Miss Abby," he says, "sounds like you've had a frightful night."

"Yes, sir." I don't know why I'm so formal. "It began with a moose."

"Began? Now this sounds like a story." He cocks his head to the side. "What does it end with?"

Now that's a question I don't have an answer to, considering my evening seems to be a work in progress.

"Wolves." Drake answers for me. "That pack that's been harrying your llamas decided to try their hand taking down a human. I tell you; the wolves are getting bolder as the seasons turn." Drake's muscles bunch beneath his snow-colored camouflage. I imagine tight corded muscle girding his frame, the perfect complement to his threatening scowl.

Unlike Bert, who's welcoming and kind, Drake's standoffish and threatening with his hardened scowl. Once again, I swallow the fear bunching in my throat. Drake terrifies me as much as he draws me to him.

Everything about him screams *Stay Away!* Yet, all I can think about is what it might feel like if I closed the distance between us.

Bert pops the cigar out of his mouth. "You found them?"

"Found and killed." Drake swings his rifle over his shoulder and puffs out his chest. "Five down. Had to leave the bodies on the side of the road, though. I should go back for them. Heard another pack on the way back. Would've gone after them except for her."

Bert shoves the fat cigar back into his mouth and draws in a breath. The tip of the cigar flares. "Don't bother. It's late. I'll call Charlie and let him know. We'll grab the wolves in the morning, send the pelts to Fish and Game, and Charlie can go after the other pack."

Drake jerks his thumb toward me. "Her Jeep is in a ditch somewhere a few miles outside of town."

"Ah, gotcha," Bert says. "I'll give Henry a call to bring his rig."

"Yeah, in the morning," Drake says.

The men exchange a look I can't decipher, but then Drake's words sink in.

"Morning!" I look between the two men. "I thought we'd be able to get it out tonight."

"Nobody's going out tonight," Drake says. "This storm's only supposed to get worse. We'll deal with it in the morning."

"Where am I going to stay?"

"She's not from around here, is she?" Bert twists the cigar in his mouth.

"Not even close." Drake surprises me with a grin. Much better than the scowl, the soft smile makes him even more handsome. His towering frame no longer feels threatening.

Instead, it's comforting.

Amazing how a simple smile transforms my rescuer.

Bert wraps an arm around my shoulder and tugs me toward the door. "Come, child, let's get you out of this weather. I've got a nice fire going and leftover stew. You look like you could use something to eat, something to drink, and some dry clothes." He glances toward Drake and the two men share another unreadable expression.

At the mention of food, my stomach rumbles. In my haste to get to Peace Springs, I skipped dinner, thinking my uncle would have something laying around. Little did I know I would nearly run down a moose and become wolf bait.

"That would be very nice, but please don't go to too much trouble."

"No trouble at all. You're in Peace Springs, child. People here take care of each other." Bert sweeps me into his home, while Drake remains outside.

I twist around. "Isn't he coming?"

Bert pulls the door shut. "Drake's going to check on the llamas, but don't worry, that brooding bastard will be back to join you by the fire in no time."

Why does the thought of sitting next to Drake by the fire have my stomach twisting in knots? Bert winks, as if he reads my mind.

He walks me through his kitchen, and unlike the man, the kitchen fits every country stereotype I can imagine. From the copper molds displayed over the cupboards, to the hen and rooster knick-knacks tucked into every available corner, there's even a wooden breadbox on the countertop. The kitchen could easily grace the cover of *Country Living* or *Southern Comfort* magazines.

Even his stove is one of those cast-iron antiques. Its jade-green metallic paint contrasts perfectly with the floral wallpaper and wooden butcher block countertops. The whole place would be terribly garish, except it all works perfectly together. It's designed to make people feel welcome.

To make them feel at home.

It also has a decidedly feminine touch to it.

The living room continues the quaint feeling, but instead of the expected plaid sofa and rocking chair with crocheted throws, the living room is the epitome of understated elegance with dark-brown leather couches and mounted gun racks over the fireplace. Unlike the kitchen, it lacks any sign of a woman's hand.

One glance at the roaring fire in the stone fireplace and I relax.

"Go ahead and make yourself comfortable. I'll heat up some stew and get you a drink. You a wine or whiskey girl?"

"Wine. I've never had whiskey." I don't take the offered seat. Instead, I reach beneath my multi-layered shirts and feel the inner-most layer. Ugh, slick with sweat. "Um, Bert, is there a place I can ..."

He points down the hall. "Bathroom is the second door on the right. The guest bedroom is the first one on the left, just across from the study."

"Thank you."

While he disappears into the kitchen, I locate the bathroom. There's no lock on the door, which makes me nervous. I take care of business and then stand in front of the mirror. A quick inspection of my ears eases my fears about frostbite.

That was too close. I thank my mysterious stranger yet again. No lingering damage will occur to my ears as a result of my rescue. My cheeks and the tip of my nose prick with sensation as circulation and heat slowly returns.

I peel out of all seven shirts. The two innermost layers are damp, but the ones in the middle are still dry. Maybe Bert has some hangers or a place where I can air out my damp clothing?

My sweats are a mess. The snow caked around my legs where it melted into the fabric. From there, it seeped into my jeans. I don't remember seeing a washer or dryer in the small country kitchen, but maybe Bert won't mind if I place my clothes by the fire. In the meantime, damp jeans it is, and I need to get out of this wet bra.

I unsnap the constricting band of fabric and hang it on the towel rack. My reflection stares back at me, rosy cheeks, pinker than the ruddy red from a few moments ago. I cup my cheeks and say a prayer of thanks. I barely missed losing the tip of my nose to frostbite. Yet another reason to thank Drake.

My hand presses against my belly as a smile escapes me.

Butterflies?

I can't remember the last time I felt butterflies.

That never happened with Scott.

The warmth of Bert's home seeps into my bones, and my shivering disappears. I toe off my wet sneakers and yank at my socks, tugging them off. Those need to dry, too. I wriggle my toes, inspecting them as well.

As I grab for one of the dry shirts, the door creaks open, making me jump. I hastily cover my chest with one of the shirts and glance down at a tabby cat rubbing up against my leg. It meows, demanding to be rubbed, which I obediently do.

I love cats, but Scott hates them. He says he has allergies, but it's a lie. There was never any eye redness, swelling, or sniffling and sneezing. It was yet another thing I gave up for the man I once loved.

"You surprised me, little kitty."

I thought I shut the door. Obviously not, because I appear to have a new friend. Deep purring vibrations fill the air as the tabby rubs against my legs.

"My, aren't you a friendly kitty?" I drape the shirt over the edge of the sink and bend down to pet the cat.

A creaking of the wood floor in the hallway startles me. I glance up at the half-open door. My gaze collides with the coal-black darkness of Drake's smoldering eyes. He takes in my naked chest and breasts, not ashamed in the least at seeing me half-naked. I squeak and grab for the shirt hanging off the sink, clutching it to my chest.

Drake doesn't react, just stands there, all six-foot-plus of him. His towering frame fills the doorway, and the heat of his eyes smolders.

My insides melt beneath his gaze, and the tiny hairs on my arms lift in response to his presence. More damning than either of those, my nipples draw tight into hard peaks.

He doesn't look away. Instead, his gaze takes a languid journey down my body then wanders up to caress my face.

Under his penetrating assessment, I freeze.

The muscles of his jaw bunch and a winter storm churns in the depths of his eyes. He takes in a sharp breath. Only then does he turn to the side and avert his gaze.

My body goes haywire in those few seconds, responding to the full force of the man standing before me, looking as if he has every right to feast upon what he sees.

He didn't look away.

Yet, it didn't feel invasive. It didn't feel wrong.

It felt all kinds of right.

He changed clothes. Tight cords rise from beneath the collar of his shirt. His Adam's apple bobs as he deliberately swallows. Ridges of muscle fill out the shirt, testing the integrity of the poor fabric as it stretches beneath the bulk of a man in the prime of his life.

My pulse thrums through my veins. A glance down reveals my failure to fully cover my breasts.

I'm giving him a peep show. Clumsily, I spread out the fabric and cover myself. My breaths huff in and out as he turns back around and transfixes me with the intensity of his gaze.

That jagged scar puckers the skin of his face. Instead of a disfigurement, it creates an aching beauty. Again, the urge to reach up and trace the lines of his pain overwhelms me, but I remember the harshness of his words earlier. My hands stay exactly where they are. The smile is gone. The scowl once again takes up residence.

"Bert thought you needed something dry to wear." His voice is deep and cautious, as unhurried as his gaze. He pushes the bathroom door until it's fully open and takes a step forward, holding out a pair of pink flannel pajamas.

One hand clutches the bunched t-shirt against my chest, while the other stretches for the clothes. Our fingers touch and the air crackles between us. I pull back as if electrified. His gaze drifts down to our fingers and his chiseled jaw tightens, turning the scowl into a grimace.

Pain flashes in his gaze.

I grab the pajamas and spin around, placing my back to him. My insides knot as tremors skate down my spine. Did I do something wrong?

"Thank you." I toss the clipped response over my left shoulder. "Did you see enough? Or are you waiting for more?"

Drake clears his throat. "I don't think it's possible to see enough. My apologies for invading your privacy, city girl." He shifts back, pivots, and heads to the living room.

I shut the door, making sure it closes this time. Only then do I look down at the clothes Drake gave me. The tabby disappeared.

Pale-pink, flannel pajamas with roses and red bows. I glance at my wet jeans and decide on comfort. Lifting the fabric to my nose, I give it a sniff, perhaps hoping to smell a little bit of him on the soft fabric.

Nothing.

When I'm dressed, I return to join the men in front of the fire.

Bert sits in the leather recliner, puffing on what looks to be a new cigar. He holds the copy of *Wuthering Heights* open by the spread of his fingers. Reading glasses perch on his nose and he strokes his bearded chin. The cat curls up on his lap.

On the coffee table, two bowls of steaming stew sit beside two empty cups and a pot of tea.

Drake sits on the sofa, a paperback clutched in his hand. From the cover, it looks to be a mystery or thriller. His gaze takes me in from head to toe, then rises again to land on my face. A storm brews in his eyes, a war in the making between desire and need, but shadows dance there as well.

Pain.

Such agony marches across his expression.

Energy pulses between us, but I'm unsure what to do about it. This kind of insane chemistry is something I've only read about.

Medically, I understand. Chemical in nature, pheromones lace the air, which brings about an intense physical attraction.

He affects a casual pose, relaxed with one leg kicked over the opposite knee, but I catch the hitching in his breath as I approach. His fingers stray up to the scar over his face, tracing out the faded lines of an old injury.

"Ah ..." Bert looks pleased with himself. "I thought Bethany's clothes would fit you." He places his book on the side table and moves the recliner to its upright position. "I hope you don't mind. Those belonged to my late wife. I'm a widower and still have a few of her things. I'm glad they fit you."

"My condolences, and thank you." I'm unsure how to respond to his statement about being a widower, or about wearing his dead wife's clothes.

This is awkward.

Bert fills in the pause of conversation. "I'm not a coffee drinker, but I made some hot tea. I've got cocoa if you'd prefer that?"

Next to the teapot and cups, two tumblers of amber-colored fluid wait.

"The tea is perfect," I say. "Thank you for your hospitality. I'm terribly sorry to be a burden."

"Child, you are no burden at all." He glances toward Drake, kicking the younger man's boot. "It's nice to have a woman over for a change, don't you agree? Isn't it nice to share the fire with Abby?"

Drake turns to Bert, a parade of emotions flashing in his expression before he schools his feelings. I bet anything he'd rather be out in that blizzard tracking down, and killing, that second pack of wolves.

Drake says nothing. He shifts in his seat, drawing his feet out of Bert's nudging distance.

I point to the glasses. "What's that?"

"Bert says you've never tasted whiskey," Drake answers.

"I prefer wine."

"Doesn't matter. In Peace Springs, we drink whiskey." Putting his book down, Drake leans forward. He grabs the two glasses and hands one to me. He taps his glass against mine. "Welcome to Peace Springs, Miss Abby ...?"

"Abby Knight." I give my full name, although I don't get the feeling Drake is happy to have me descending on his small town. Then he surprises me, rewarding me with one of his elusive smiles.

"Now that is a pretty name." He presses the cup to his lips and tilts his head back, downing the entire glass in one swallow. Despite the smile, the hardness of his eyes returns, glittering as he waits for me to drink my whiskey.

I sniff the aromatic liquor. It's far stronger than wine. The alcohol burns the sensitive tissues of my nose, but it smells like heaven. I tip the glass against my lips, coating them in whiskey. Then I lick my lips, closing my eyes when a sweet flavor coats my tongue.

"What kind of whiskey is this?" It's nothing like I expected. There's a burn, of course, but an amazingly mature flavor coats my tongue.

Drake pours himself another drink. "Salted caramel whiskey, a good starter drink." His eyes lock onto my mouth as I lick my lips. "We'll work you up to the harder stuff over time."

I take another sip. "It's like wine, with all the different flavors, but unique and distinct."

Then his words hit, *over time*? He's thinking about other times.

As in *more* than tonight.

Is he interested in seeing me after tonight? Boy, I hope so.

That thought makes the butterflies in my belly take flight, and while I'd like to think the whiskey is what heats my cheeks, I know that's a lie. Deep down, I very much want to see more of Drake.

Which is crazy. I'm in no position to be thinking about starting up anything with anyone.

Especially after the disaster with Scott. I can't believe he thinks I'll ever go back to him.

"Do you like?" Drake watches me closely.

Another sip, this one bigger than the previous one. The burn of alcohol lights a fire inside my mouth and coats my throat with a delicious burn.

"Oh my, that's strong stuff." I cough and sputter.

Drake smiles, then turns to Bert. "I think we have a convert."

"Seems so." Bert barely follows our conversation. He's become one with his chair and turns a page in his book.

Drake picks up a bowl and hands it to me.

"Eat," he orders. "You've had a hard night."

The ceramic fills my palm with warmth, while the steam carries the savory aromas of the stew to my nose. Without warning, my stomach rumbles.

With a laugh, Drake sits back on the couch, cradling his bowl in his massive hand. Dipping a spoon in the thick mixture of meat and vegetables, he blows at the surface to cool off the stew before taking a bite. I join him on the couch, tucking my legs beneath me as I take another sniff.

"It smells heavenly. Thank you." It doesn't take long to empty my bowl. With a yawn, I stretch.

Bert lifts his nose out of his book and glances at me. "You ready to hit the sack?"

"I can't thank you enough for your hospitality."

"Drake," Bert says. "Why don't you show your city girl to your room?"

Drake stands. His towering presence causes me to catch my breath. He collects our bowls and carries them into the kitchen. My whiskey glass sits on the side table, empty.

I took my time drinking it, savoring the sweet burn. My face feels flushed from the alcohol, a welcome change from the burning sensation of near frostbite.

A strange twisting knots my stomach when Drake returns. I don't understand why my pulse quickens or my breathing hitches, but something about him unsettles me on a gut level.

"Come," he says, and then heads down the hall to the first door on the left.

Opening the door, he gestures for me to go inside. I step through and stop short at a pair of twin beds.

Surely Drake won't be sleeping in the same room as me?

He waits while I approach the far bed and crawl under the covers. Once I pull the sheets up to my neck, he flicks off the light and closes the door.

That's when I realize the man literally 'put me to bed.'

Warm and soft, the flannel bedsheets suck me into a blissfully relaxed state where thoughts of moose, snow, and wolves become a distant memory. In their place, images of a man with raven hair, and even blacker eyes, fill my dreams.

5

BACON

I have no idea when I fell asleep or even when Drake went to bed. He isn't in the room when I wake, but he clearly slept in the other twin bed. The sheets are a rumpled mess, and there is a clear indentation of his head on the pillow.

I shared a room with a man I barely know and lived to talk about it. This weird feeling inside of me, the one that says I wish something had happened last night, doesn't belong to me.

I'm sensible, not reckless. Meaning, I don't hop into bed with strangers. Although, it seems I evidently sleep in the same room with one.

Emphasis on *sleep*.

My approach to relationships, quoting Scott, is *ponderous*.

Relationship?

Boy, does that feel way too soon.

Impulsive is not an adjective to describe me, but damn if I don't want to be a bit reckless with Drake.

A man I know nothing about.

I did look for a ring around his finger last night. No ring. No indentation of a recently removed ring. That doesn't mean he's available, but at least there's no wife, or a recent ex-wife to deal with.

His stares feel interested. He wouldn't check me out like that if he isn't open for something to happen.

Right?

Did I sleep so soundly that I missed him crawling into the other bed?

Did he change clothes? Strip down to his skivvies and slide under the covers? *Skivvies*, it's a fun word, one my father used often. A smile curves my lips for a moment with fond memories of my father, but as soon as the smile appears, heartache and a frown steal it away.

As far as Drake's sleeping attire, I'm keenly interested in what he wore to bed. I tend to sleep in a t-shirt and panties. Last night, I wore flannel pj's. Did he, similarly, wear far more to bed than usual because we shared a room? Or does he sleep in the nude?

Here I am crushing on the man who rescued me last night when there's probably nothing more than an element of chivalry going on. Like some part of small-town values that I've never experienced in the hustle and bustle of the suburban corridor which feeds Los Angeles.

I'm ashamed to realize that and feel foolish for letting my imagination run wild.

Honestly, this is the kind of life I want to live—small town, family values. To depend on your neighbors and trust strangers. That should be how everything is in life.

Unfortunately, that isn't the way things are where I grew up. In Redlands, we don't trust strangers. We barely know our neighbors. I never walked alone at night, and I always checked the locks and set the alarm before going to bed.

Memories of Redlands don't come without mention of Scott: the man who promised to love and cherish me but demeaned me with his words and subdued me with his fists.

To think I almost married Scott.

What a mistake that would've been.

When I ripped off the engagement ring and flung it at him, Scott caught the two-carat diamond. His entire demeanor shifted, thrumming with the anger flooding his body. I grabbed Boston, my poor beleaguered fern, and ran to my car. As I drove off, his shouts sent icy tendrils down my spine.

"You'll be back, and you'd better not make me come find you." My shoulders lift as a flood of pain and regret run through me. Best not to think about Scott.

Besides, I'd rather get back to thinking about Drake and the whole sleeping in the same room thing.

What did he wear to bed?

Not that I'm on the market.

Far from it.

I'm so far *off* the market I don't even know where Market Street is.

Why do I care?

Once again, I'm not looking at hopping into another relationship after the catastrophic fallout from the one I barely escaped, but that doesn't mean I'm oblivious to whether a man might be interested.

The reason I obsess has nothing to do with Drake and everything to do with the fear I'll never find my *one*.

With medical school and residency, the years are piling up behind me. I'll be thirty in a couple of years. If I don't find my *one* by then, I'll be in my thirties when I have kids.

The one thing my parents stressed when we talked about the future was how important it was to spend the first few years of a marriage as a couple. Adding kids into the mix too soon, according to them, doesn't give a new couple enough time to get to know each other.

Kids stress a marriage.

I didn't appreciate hearing that—seeing how I'm their only child—but I've seen it in my medical practice. I've seen young couples getting pregnant. After I deliver their babies, stress builds. Doing the math, I'll be in my late thirties before thinking about kids. As a doctor, I know complication rates skyrocket for women in their late thirties.

Why am I thinking about babies?

How did I get down this path? All I want to know is whether Drake's attracted to me.

Can I even do the dating thing again? It's been so long since I've made myself available. What if I forgot how?

The thing is, I want Drake to like me. I need it for personal validation that Scott didn't steal my best years.

Drake interests me. From his no-nonsense air to the imperfections of that scar, I want to know everything about him. But I'm keenly aware of my deficits when it comes to men. History shows I'm a poor judge of character.

My focus should be on what matters. That's establishing myself as the new town doctor, working alongside my uncle until he retires. Then, I'll be *the* town doctor with all the responsibility that comes with that designation.

I need to give the townspeople reason to trust me and that doesn't happen by sleeping my way through the town's eligible bachelors from day one.

Not that I'm that kind of girl, but my point's made. As far as my deficits go, I'm an incredibly poor judge of character.

I never saw the abuse coming from Scott.

That's what bothers me the most.

Too caught up in the illusion of love, I missed every warning sign. From Scott's overprotectiveness to his jealous rages, I excused every instance of Scott's instability.

I forgave every hit, every punch, and continued to lie to myself as I sat in the emergency room with cracked ribs, swollen lips, and bruises that covered every square inch of my body. He made me believe it was my fault.

I knew better. Yet, I still believed the lie he forced me to accept. That's what I hate the most.

I'm a smart woman.

A professional.

I'm trained in how to recognize and treat domestic abuse.

Yet, I still believed I was at fault.

These thoughts are too heavy for the morning. I need to think of lighter things, more important things. Things like getting my Jeep out of that ditch and letting my uncle know where I am.

I stretch, luxuriating in the softness of the flannel sheets and quilted coverlet. My toes, fingers, nose, and ears pulse with heat.

Sunlight streaks through the lace curtains, and I blink away the sleep from my eyes. My lips curl into a slow smile.

The feeling of being home settles deep within my chest. I twist side-to-side, loosening my back and stretching my neck, enjoying the slow process of waking up.

Nose twitching, I catch the faint aroma of breakfast drifting down the hall from the kitchen. Is that what woke me? I sniff again, and this time a broad smile curves my lips.

Bacon!

6

BREAKFAST

THE WARM, SIZZLING SCENT OF BACON BRINGS BACK MEMORIES OF MY mother's cooking, making the room smell like a lazy Sunday sleep-in kind of day, with a whole lot of awesome heaped on top.

Maybe Peace Springs isn't so bad after all?

As much as I want to stay in bed and soak up the warm feeling, I need to get up and greet my hosts. Swinging my feet around, a neatly folded stack of clothes catches my eye.

My clothes.

They sit on the nightstand beside my bed. Did Bert wash and dry my clothes while I slept?

Or was it Drake?

A glance toward the door confirms it's shut, but after the bathroom incident last night, I pad over and check to make sure it's securely latched. A few minutes later, I have both beds made and I've changed into my jeans. This time, I only put one shirt on, instead of seven.

My teeth feel fuzzy, and the fullness of my bladder pinches. Opening the door, I peek into the hallway, looking toward the living room. Male voices echo down the hall, originating from the kitchen.

It's the deep kind of laughter of two men who know each other well. It rumbles through the house, warming it from the inside out.

I tiptoe to the bathroom, relieve myself, and then finger-scrub the fuzz away from my teeth. I check myself in the mirror, paying special attention to my ears, nose, and even my cheeks. Despite my ordeal, I made it through the blizzard without any damage.

But I've stalled long enough.

Drake's voice bounces off the walls, deep and resonating; it tunnels beneath my skin and slams into my gut, twisting and knotting into a tangled mess. My belly flutters and my breaths turn shallow. Rapid. Nervous to see him again.

When I enter the kitchen, both men turn at the same time. Drake holds a spatula and stands in front of the cast-iron stove. A skillet sizzles and pops as bacon crisps in its grease. Bert stands at the counter, a white and blue striped ceramic bowl cradled in the crook of his arm. He beats at the contents with a wire whisk.

"Good morning, sunshine." Bert's bright smile welcomes me yet again, making me feel at home. "Sleep well?"

"I did, thank you."

Drake's gaze rakes over my body, taking in every inch and lingers longer than is polite. Unlike Bert's bright and cheery welcome, Drake's attention is something else entirely.

The dark, sweltering heat simmering in his eyes speeds my heart and deepens my breaths. The loose-fitting faded pair of jeans fails to conceal his physique composed of tight cords and hard ridges of defined muscle.

His poor t-shirt stretches across broad shoulders, and I have no doubt it hides a rippling terrace of muscle underneath. The man exudes power. His threatening scowl does nothing to soften those hard edges. Too much pain laces that scowl, and I can't help but want to ease some of the agony, which seems to be such an integral part of his makeup.

He's well-built without being overly muscular, unlike the gym die-hards who flood the local gyms back in Redlands. I signed up a time or two, thinking the addition of a bit of gym time would help me lose the extra five pounds Scott always went on and on about. After my first visit, with powerlifters and bulky men amped up on protein powder and questionably legal substances, I never returned.

Drake's muscular build appears to be the result of honest to goodness labor, working the land.

My gaze dips, following the narrowing of his waist to the V-cut indentations I know are hidden under the fabric. His pants outline just enough of a bulge to fire up my pulse again. No man has a right to look that good.

His raven-black hair, long on the top and short on the sides, flops over his eyes in a disheveled mess. As I stare, he rakes his fingers through the messy strands, pushing the hair out of his eyes. It immediately falls back, as rebellious and untamed as I imagine he must be.

I try to determine his age. He's older than me, but how much older? From the lack of wrinkles on his face, I guess a year or two at most. Maybe three or five. But his piercing gaze wears authority with ease. It makes me wonder if he's prior military.

Maybe the scar is the result of an injury obtained while on active duty? That could explain the maturity I sense. There's nothing left of the youth he once was. Some tragedy stripped that innocence.

Everything about Drake screams, "stay away." There's a wildness to his features that can't be denied. There's also pain, terrible agony etched in the hardness of his features.

I'm staring, but I can't look away. He regards me silently, allowing my intrusive gaze to get its fill, and he doesn't flinch beneath my scrutiny. At least, not until I wonder about that scar.

Standing feet braced, shoulder-width apart, he's intimidating, but the moment my focus shifts to the scar, he turns back to the stove.

Bert catches every nuance. His inquisitive gaze flickers between us, bouncing back and forth until our entirely silent exchange concludes with Drake giving me his back.

Which doesn't help my predicament at all.

Now I've got nothing better to look at than the way Drake's tight ass fills out those jeans. Everything about this mysterious man conjures the most decadent and indecent thoughts. There's a ruthlessness about him, a carnal need vibrating in the tenseness of his tall, muscular form.

It's volatile.

He's dangerous, but damn, if that doesn't make me want to take a walk on the wild side. Which screams trouble with a capital T.

Fortunately for me, I'm not the kind of girl who makes the first move. I'm far too timid for that. Now, my imagination, on the other hand, already has our bodies twisting and tangling, skin sliding against skin, and other parts of our bodies locked in an intimate embrace.

"How do you like your eggs, city girl?" Drake's velvety baritone sends shivers of sensation racing along my skin.

My veins hum with a flickering heat, but I try to sound nonchalant as if his presence doesn't do strange things to my body. "Over medium, please." My gut simmers with the low grunt he returns.

"Breakfast will be done shortly," he says. "Why don't you relax in the living room? We'll call you."

"Is there something I can help with?"

Bert keeps whipping the batter, attention shifting between me and Drake, while the focus of my attention slowly turns back around.

"We've got this, city girl. I'll call you when it's time." Drake dismisses me with callous disregard, leaving me unsure what I should do with myself.

Having two men labor over my breakfast is a decadence I'm not accustomed to

but will gladly enjoy. Even if I feel a little guilty snuggling into the warm leather of Bert's couch instead of setting the table or helping in some other way.

A few minutes later, Bert calls me in. The round kitchen table is set, and I join them for the best eggs, bacon, and pancakes I've ever had.

"Thank you, that was delicious." My voice cracks as I stand and try to clear the dishes.

"I've got KP duty." Bert rises, taking the dishes out of my hands. "Why don't you help Drake with the chores outside while I clean up in here? Henry won't be around for another hour, and I'm sure Drake will appreciate your help." He walks over to a closet and pulls out a coat. "Here, you can borrow this. It was Bethany's."

With the exception of the kitchen, there's a definite lack of feminine presence in the home, but he still keeps some of her things. How long ago did she die? It's a shame because Bert looks like the kind of man who is desperately in love with his wife. I bet he misses her terribly, but I don't voice my thoughts. He reminds me a little of my uncle, who lost my aunt several years ago. There's a lingering sadness, which never fully goes away.

"Thank you." I take the coat from Bert.

Drake unfolds his long, lean frame from the chair, and my eyes cut to the flex of his biceps. I touch my fingers to my neck where my pulse races beneath the pad of my finger. Reluctantly, I drag my attention from Drake's impressive form as he shrugs into his jacket and turns back around. He snatches the coat from my hands, shakes it out, and holds it for me.

He crowds my personal space while I shove first one arm and then the other inside the borrowed coat. When I pull at the bottom to zip it up, Drake places his hands on my shoulders and unceremoniously spins me around. His towering frame puts me eye level with his chest. I'm used to Scott's much shorter stature and being eye-to-eye. With Drake, all I see is the expanse of his chest.

While he zips me into the coat, no part of him actually touches me. It's as if he tries not to touch me, but if he doesn't want to touch me, why is he in my space?

My entire body reacts to the nearness of him. His dark, masculine scent floods my nostrils as I fill my lungs. His words about *zip it, don't sniff it* pass through my thoughts, and I can't help my bite down on my lower lip to keep from giggling like a lunatic.

He pulls the zipper all the way up my chest, snugging it below my chin. Bending closer, he inspects his handiwork, then cocks his head to the side.

"You ready to see the llamas?"

7

BARN

A SMILE WORKS AT THE CORNERS OF DRAKE'S EYES, AND I WONDER IF HE didn't just sniff me. The gravelly intonations of his voice will be my undoing. I just know it. No one should sound that sexy.

His raven-black hair falls across his brow, perfectly unruly and disheveled. He finger-combs it back into place, where it stays for a moment, only to fall across his eyes again.

The scar on his face draws my attention, a ragged line extending over the left side of his face. It must have been painful, and I wonder how he got it.

His eyes pinch, perhaps noticing my focus on the disfigurement.

I clear my throat and inject cheer into my voice. "I'd love to see the llamas."

His eyes lock with mine. Strange how much power radiates from those depths. I wish I could see his pupils, but they're indistinguishable from the dark rims of his irises.

Drake dips his head and opens the back door, sweeping his arm outward. I take his lead and step into the chilly morning air while ignoring how his sculpted lips tip upward into a smirk.

This man will be my undoing. My insides warm with the sound of his voice. My steps lighten with the solid tread of his steps behind me. The brutal beauty of his face, punctuated by that puckered and ragged scar, speak to torment, agony, and survival.

He stands behind me, close enough to feel the heat of his breaths on the back of my neck. It's unsettling enough that I grab at my hair and free it from the messy bun. As I shake out the long strands, a strangled sound comes from Drake. He places a hand on the small of my back, steering me toward the barn.

"It's beautiful out here." I can't help but stop and take in the beauty all around me.

Instead of darkness and fear, I'm greeted with the light of a new day and all the hope that comes with it.

Overhead, the deepest blue greets the day. Over the ridge, the sun begins its steady climb skyward. There isn't a cloud in the sky. Not a single speck from the storm of the previous evening. And it's warmer than I expect.

My breath isn't visible, and my hands don't ache from the cold. Beneath my feet, wet snow crunches as it melts beneath the dawning sun.

I found my sneakers drying by the fire in the living room. Bert's hospitality is beyond thoughtful. They'll be wet again soon with the melting snow, but I no longer fear hypothermia, frostbite, and death.

As far as my eye can see, a blanket of white sparkles under the morning sun. I fight against the urge to spin in a circle, arms stretched wide, taking in the scene.

"Beyond gorgeous." Drake's hard gaze locks on my face.

My cheeks heat because he's not talking about the farm.

"Come." He turns toward the barn as my insides heat.

It's one word. An order given to follow. But it's more than that. Something carnal stirs in his voice: a promise for something more.

I follow him in companionable silence, broken only by the crunching of snow beneath our feet. At the barn, he unlatches the massive doors, then puts his back into sliding them on their rails until a narrow gap appears. He holds the doors open with the brace of his arm.

As I pass beneath his arm, the heat of his breath sears my skin and makes me shiver. My breath flees me as I pry my gaze from his hooded eyes to take in the dimly lit interior of the barn.

Musk, a deep, animal smell, fills the air. The pungent aroma of dirt, hay, and what must be llamas assaults my nostrils. An odd, low hum vibrates in the air. I feel it more than hear it. It's practically subsonic. I cast my gaze left and right until I realize the sound is coming from a pen to my left.

"What is that?" I ask.

Drake chuckles. "Llamas humming."

"That noise is from them?"

"If you like their humming, you should hear the males orgle." Mischief sparks in his voice.

"Did you just make up that word?" I arch my brow, thinking he's pulling the wool over my eyes.

"No."

When he laughs, his dark hair falls forward again. He reaches up, pushing the hair off his face, and draws my attention back to the scar.

"I hate to ask, but what's an orgle?"

I'm going to regret asking, but how can I not? Orgle is no word I've ever heard of before. I swear Drake's making it up.

"Llamas hum when they're happy. The males have a unique alarm call when they perceive danger, but when they breed, they orgle."

"Breed?"

"Yes." His low chuckle shouldn't be as sexy as it is, but heat fills my cheeks and butterflies flutter in my stomach.

"Orgle?"

"Yes, but it's not breeding season, just the humming for right now." His eyes crinkle at the corners. "I bet you're dying to hear a llama orgle now, aren't you?"

He steps close, towering over me, causing a tingle to spark in my chest and an ache to build lower down. My entire body is painfully aware of his overwhelming presence.

The timbre of his voice is both smooth and hypnotic, drugging even, because I find myself tipping my head back and closing my eyes as he leans down.

His breath disturbs the air above my cheek, and I hold still, paralyzed by what might happen next.

"What are you doing to me, city girl?" He touches a knuckle to my chin. His voice grows tight, hoarse, and needy.

"I'm not ..." But my heart lifts at this unexpected turn of events.

He's close. Closer than he's ever been, crowding my space as the heat of his breaths fan across my face. His rich, deep scent fills my senses.

It's carnal and raw.

Seductive and exotic.

It's unlike anything I've experienced before.

"Shh." He brushes a finger over the fullness of my lips.

My eyes widen, and my lips part in breathless anticipation. Drake backs me up against the barn wall. My shoulders touch the rough pine siding as he cages me in.

I stare into the brutal, mesmerizing beauty of his face as the pad of his thumb brushes across the seam of my lips. I must be out of my mind because my lips part.

He bends over me, torso tight, muscles vibrating with need. I stare into the arresting imperfection of his face and dive into the dark pools of desire swimming in his eyes.

He's a strong, powerful man. Big enough to force me against my will. Perhaps I was too trusting coming out here alone with him?

But, isn't this what I want?

I wish I had an answer to that. Coming to Peace Springs is a way for me to start over, but I'm not looking to jump into a new relationship.

Work is my focus.

Or should be. Yet, here I am.

Alone.

In a barn.

With a man who rescued me from wolves and worse. He brought me to safety.

This is when I should make a break for it, but I find myself entranced and hope he'll deliver on the promise smoldering in his gaze.

Every nerve in my body stands up and takes notice, thrumming with anticipation as he dips his head and lowers his mouth.

"You're a provocative and intoxicating mystery that kept me up all night."

His seductive voice transfixes me. It's deep and rumbles with all the power and promise of a distant thunderstorm on the horizon.

I could run for shelter. Or, I can take a risk and weather the full force of the storm as it descends upon me. Is this what I want? Am I too scarred from Scott and the cruelty of his fists to trust another man?

I don't want to be that person. I want to believe in a world where kindness and good prevail. I want to believe in men like Drake who rescue those in danger and provide them shelter from the storm.

Is that too much to ask?

"I didn't ..."

He taps the pad of his thumb against my lips.

"My dreams were positively indecent." He captures my eyes with his stormy gaze. "What are you doing to me?"

"I'm not ..."

"You are, and you feel it too." His stony gaze shifts from my face to the rest of me. "I feel it in you."

"Drake, I don't know about ..."

He silences me with a sharp shake of his head.

"I'm going to say this only once, and I don't mean it to frighten you, but I need you to understand."

"Understand, what?" I'm so overwhelmed right now he could recite gibberish and I wouldn't know the difference.

"When I see something I want, there's very little to stop me from going after it. If you don't want this to go any further, I need you to tell me no. I'll take a step back. I'll walk away, but—this is your one and only warning. I want you, city girl. I want you in ways that are positively indecent."

My heart sputters as his brick-hard body moves closer. He's everywhere all at once.

The press of his body.

The heat of his breath.

The low rumble of his voice.

Drake cages me in. His breath rustles my hair as he dips his head, not for the kiss I desire, but to nuzzle my neck. He hooks an arm around my waist and pulls me against his body.

I let my gaze flit, bouncing from the ceiling to the dark depths of the interior of the barn, until it finally settles on the stubble of his jaw.

He doesn't wait for me to answer, but crowds me in, towering over me.

"I really hope you say yes, city girl." He threads his fingers through the length of my hair, grasping the strands as his lips hover, a kiss away. "But you can say no. I'll never make you do something you don't want to do."

His need whispers through me, potent, powerful, and raw. Then he shifts, touching our foreheads together as if he has all the time in the world to let this moment hang between us. For a man who says he's not a patient man, he sure is letting this moment linger.

It's intoxicating, wholly unexpected, deliciously raw, and absolutely carnal.

Primal.

His fingers glide to my neck.

"If you don't want this, say no." His gruff tone catches me off guard. "Because I'm not going to stop if you say yes."

What do I want? I don't know anything about Drake, except our connection grows stronger with each beat of my heart. The seconds lengthen with me too tongue-tied to say what's on my mind.

He saved me from certain death, but am I ready to hop into bed with another man? Is that what we're talking about? A quick romp in the hay?

And then what?

It would be fun, and to be honest, I kind of need that sort of validation after what I've been through. Except, I'm not a one-and-done kind of girl.

I wish I were.

Hell, I wish I was with Drake, but I'm leery of giving in too soon, too fast.

Too easy.

But what if this is exactly what I need? A bit of distraction from the pain filling my past?

One of my reasons for coming to Peace Springs is to make a fresh start. To leave the pain of broken promises and flying fists behind me, where they can't hurt me anymore, but I have no intention of jumping into another relationship.

My answer hovers on the next breath. And I don't know what I'll say.

8

WELCOME

A GROAN RUMBLES THROUGH DRAKE'S CHEST, A LOW, WARBLING SOUND full of masculine need. His desire echoes in the hammering of my pulse. This connection we share doesn't make sense.

It's insane. Intense.

We barely know each other.

We met less than twelve hours ago, but whatever *this* is, it isn't something I want to stop.

I lick my lips, wetting them in preparation for the heat of his mouth upon me. With a shuddering inhale, I glide my fingers across the swell of his biceps and sweep across the hardened planes of his chest. My fingers explore every ridge and valley of his sharply cut muscle.

I stroke the back of his neck and twine my fingers in the hair at his nape. He's tall, broad of shoulder, and can't help but dominate my personal space. Normally, that's something I would avoid.

How many times did Scott cage me in?

That never ended well.

This, however, is different in so many ways. Most importantly, I welcome the intrusion. I *want* to see where this leads.

My lungs seethe with my answer, hanging on the precipice of saying, if not *yes*, then definitely not the *no* he demands.

As reckless as this is, being with Drake feels like coming home. Or maybe, it feels like closing the door on my past.

With my lips parted, I rise on tiptoe, eliminating that final gap between us. Brushing our lips together, I seal my fate.

"I don't want you to stop."

Simple, raw desire flares in his gaze as he seizes my mouth with a guttural groan. There's nothing coy or teasing about his assault. No gentle gliding of his lips against mine or easy exploration with his tongue.

Drake seals our lips, pulling me hard against him. He pushes in with his tongue, claiming and taking, pillaging and plundering. The unexpectedness of it sweeps me off my feet. His entire body vibrates with male arousal: a primal reaction, which sets my nerves on fire.

I should be surprised, but he warned me he wouldn't be gentle.

His kiss isn't the tender exploration of first-time lovers. There's no hesitancy. He's primal, primitive even, frenzied in his need to take and claim.

I surrender to his need, inviting him in, accepting the brutality of his desire with an answering urgency of my own. He takes from me with bruising aggression, his tongue demanding and determined, while I lift up on tiptoe and wrap my hands around his neck.

I've never been kissed like this before. It's as if he puts his whole body, his entire soul, into the act of sealing our lips and joining our bodies. If this is the way he kisses—what will the rest of it feel like?

Once he breaches my defenses, his tongue chases mine. His lips fortify his attack with a firm, combative strength against my yielding acquiescence. His reckless hunger surprises me, but that's nothing compared to my response.

I become something unfamiliar.

Something wild and untamed.

Feral in my need, a hunger wakes within me, demanding and raw.

Or maybe I simply need one man to replace the pain of another?

Whatever my motivation, Drake is here, and my ex is quickly becoming nothing more than a painful memory.

This kiss is everything.

It's powerful enough to cause serious damage because I realize a painful truth. I can fall for a man like Drake. With every nerve in my body thrumming with the punishing strokes of his tongue, I burn beneath the unrestrained wildness of his desire.

My exhales turn erratic, quickening with the speed of his assault. His hot mouth and talented tongue are more experienced than my tentative response. He licks and nips, driving me insane as he dominates the space we share with his overwhelming presence.

His kiss is unlike anything I've ever dreamed about. It's beyond what I thought possible. The relentless demands of his mouth steadily sweep me off my feet.

My entire body trembles as I tilt my head back to beg for more. I swallow a needy moan as my left leg lifts, wrapping around his hip, needing to climb his towering frame and take this to its logical conclusion.

Drake palms my ass and lifts me against his groin, where he grinds against me, showing me the depth of his arousal. A groan drives his hips harder as we shamelessly grind against one another while his mouth punishes my swollen lips.

My blood warms, liquid heat courses through my veins, melting me from the inside out. I squirm against him as my hot, itchy nerves demand more.

More heat. More friction. More of him and his touch.

Our clothing becomes our enemy, preventing us from feeling skin on skin. My nipples tighten and my inner thighs pulse, awakening a needful ache in my core.

And this is just a kiss.

The punishing rhythm doesn't give me time to think or agonize over thoughts of what I want to come next. I surrender myself to the moment, content to let it last forever.

And while I lose myself under the torment of his kiss, my heart sputters as it wakes from a self-imposed slumber. Shell-shocked to silence after the ordeal I left in Redlands, California, it wakens and comes alive.

His mouth floats over mine. His hot breath fans my face. Placing both hands on my ass, he pulls me close while I shamelessly wrap my leg around his hip, grinding against him.

Drake yanks me off my feet, drawing my legs around his hips. He holds me with ease as our mouths war with each other and our tongues tangle in a maddening dance.

My tongue darts out, seeking his, as my head slants for more, giving him full access to what he needs. He tightens his grip and rocks me against his hardness.

Friction.

I need more of that friction. His razor-like teeth grip my lower lip, biting down until I gasp with a pinch of pain.

"I told you, I'm not gentle, city girl. You'll have marks before we're done. You've been warned," he growls.

No shit, I've been warned.

I want more of this and release one hand from his neck. Shaking my arm, I manage to yank it out of the sleeve of the heavy coat. Drake sees what I'm doing and helps me with the other arm. The coat falls to the floor, where it lands gently on the straw-covered floor of the barn.

I push the collar of Drake's jacket back, exposing his shoulders. Together, we manage to get first one arm and then his other free. His jacket joins mine.

His mouth glides against mine, his tongue lashing, furious and determined. I crack open my lids and peek at the pinch of his dark brows. His expression tightens with the urgency of his need, and while he cups my face, he drives me to combustion.

Then his words sink in.

Heart racing, I pause. Is this what I want? A one-night stand with a stranger?

My nerves riot, sparking with warring desire. My palm drifts to his chest, crushed between the press of our bodies. The hard terrace of his muscles vibrates beneath my fingers. A fever spreads through me, the need to feel all of him goes to battle against my rational mind, which tells me to stomp on the brakes.

He pulls back, his strong arms holding me firmly in place. Only the fabric of our clothes separates us from a more carnal union. What terrifies me most is how much my body aches to make that happen.

The rumble of a truck sounds outside; something big and heavy, with a rattling of chains.

"Damn." Drake pulls away with a growl. "Henry's early." A smile curves his lips, "City girl, you know how to make a man ache in the best possible way."

He lifts me off his hips and places me on the ground, holding me steady until I find my balance. His head cants to the side, studying me. "You're nothing like what I expected."

"What did you expect?"

"Cold and frigid came to mind when we met. You were a bit prickly."

"Prickly?" I take a step back. "Did you just call me frigid?"

Drake's hand whips forward, grabbing my wrist. He pulls me back into his arms. "That mind of yours thinks too much. You asked me a question, and I answered honestly, but you didn't let me finish."

"You said I was frigid and prickly."

"I sure did, but I wasn't the only one interested in taking that kiss a whole lot further. For the record, I'm assuming you weren't at your best last night. Freezing, facing down a pack of wolves, and hiking all that way in sneakers ..." He tilts my chin, forcing me to face him. "My first impression changed the moment you followed me. You were totally out of your element, but you never once complained. Most women would've bitched about how difficult that hike was, but you didn't. That's when I knew ..."

9

FRIGID

DRAKE'S LOW, HUSKY LAUGH MAKES IT IMPOSSIBLE TO STAY ANGRY. NOT that I am. The heat of our kiss still lingers between us. My entire body wants more. It's too late to pretend I didn't want a whole lot more to happen after that kiss.

Drake's words swirl in my mind.

Frigid is a word Scott used. Generally, it was followed by a lesson delivered beneath a torrent of his fists.

"Knew, what?" My entire body shakes, waiting for Drake to respond.

"I decided you were the kind of woman I needed to get to know better. It's why I told Bert to have Henry come today instead of last night."

"Wait. Henry could have come last night? I didn't have to stay the night?"

"If Henry had come, he would've taken you away from me. I wasn't ready for that to happen. At least, not until I had a chance to see what you were really like."

"We didn't exactly spend a lot of time together. You put me to bed after finishing that stew. If you wanted to get to know me better ..."

"Luv, you were exhausted. After that whiskey got into your

system, your lids kept bouncing closed." The corner of his mouth ticks up in a grin. "Can I say sleeping in the same room with you was torture? I went to bed hard and woke up hard. You, my dear," he taps the tip of my nose, "are achingly beautiful. You're tough as nails, and I find that sexy as shit."

"I can't believe you did that." I put my hands on my hips. "You lied to me."

"I made a decision that was in the best interests of everyone involved."

"How so?"

"First off, it would've put Henry out coming all this way to get you last night, and with the snow still falling, not to mention *not knowing* where your car might be, I figured why do that to him? Much easier to find your car in daylight. You were safe, and I needed more time to see the real you, instead of the scared, terrified, out of your element, you."

"I feel like I should be really mad at you about now." The key word being *should*, but I'm not mad at all. I'm incredibly touched.

"Probably, but it all turned out for the best."

"How's that?"

"Because that kiss knocked you off your feet." His grin turns into a smirk. "My plan worked out just the way it needed to. Now, I know I'll see you again. We're finishing what we started. It's just a matter of when."

"Is that so?" I stare up at him, trying to be stern with him, but his grin brings a smile to my face.

"Tell me that kiss didn't rock your world." He grabs me around the waist and yanks me against him, letting the long, hard length of him press against my belly. "I'm so hard right now, city girl, I can barely think. My dick is going to drill a hole in my pants."

"You're not exactly shy."

"Why bother beating around the bush? I wanted to kiss you, so I did. I want to fuck you, and I will." Drake releases me. "Just not right now."

"You sure don't beat around the bush." My fingers lift to press against my swollen lips.

A horn honks outside.

I'm not ready to leave. Drake is cocky as shit. I love it. And I definitely want to see him again. He played me, maneuvering me right where he wanted. I give him points for being so damn slick about it.

"Why waste time when we're grown, consenting adults. I told you I'm not a gentle man. I'm also not slow when I find a woman who interests me. This thing between us, city girl, it's only just beginning."

Henry leans on the horn, demanding our attention.

I bend down and grab the jacket Bert loaned me. While dusting off straw and dirt, the chill in the air seems to magically reappear. A few seconds ago, my entire body heated with passion. Now, the crisp morning air reminds me this is Montana in May instead of Redlands, where the temperatures start pegging triple digits by now.

He leans down and kisses my brow, a slow sensual press of his lips and a promise for more. "Consider this your reprieve. Next time, there's no way I'm stopping at a simple kiss."

Only there was nothing simple about that kiss.

"Bert!" A deep voice yells outside. "Drake!" Snow crunches under the weight of heavy boots. "You guys around?"

Drake presses his lips against mine, a soft, gentle caress, more damaging than our first kiss because, in that moment, he cements his promise to make me his.

"In here," he calls out. "Henry, we're in here."

Grasping my hand in his, he shrugs into his jacket and pulls me outside. The blaze of the morning sun beats down on the snow, melting it. It's only a few degrees above freezing, nothing like the nearly sub-zero temperatures of last night.

The corners of my lips turn up when I spy Henry. I suffer from the same preconceived notions about the tow truck driver that I did with Bert. But I giggle because Henry is the epitome of my stereotype.

With his grease-stained overalls, blue and white plaid shirt, and heavy boots, he has a stem of hay firmly planted between his teeth. The only thing he doesn't have is the cowboy hat. Instead, he wears a black knit beanie pulled down over his ears. His expression brightens when he catches sight of me. He gives a long, low, whistle.

Drake squeezes my hand and pulls me close to his side.

"Henry Watkins, meet Abby Knight."

My heart stumbles to a halt. That is the first time Drake has said my name, and the low rumble of possession falters my step.

Ignoring the odd range of emotions flowing through my mind, I focus on Henry. "Thank you for coming out to help me."

Henry pulls off his cap, revealing a bald head. "Pleasure's all mine. Heard you ran into a ditch."

"It seemed better than running into the moose."

"Oh, glad you didn't do that. Deer are bad enough. Plenty of them around here. A deer can take out your bumper, maybe your hood, but a moose? Them suckers can crack an engine block. Kill you and them both. I'm surprised, to be honest. We don't usually get moose around here. Must've been driven out of the mountains by the storm."

"Oh." I didn't realize they were that dangerous.

"You ready to get your car?" Henry asks.

I glance at Drake. I want to head back into that barn. Then, I remember something important.

"I forgot to call my uncle. I told him to expect me late last night, and now I feel horrible." It didn't occur to me last night to call. Drake affected me that strongly. Uncle Pete is probably worried sick. "I need to call my uncle and let him know I'm okay."

"We can call him on the way." Henry opens the door to his tow rig. I turn when it looks like Drake isn't going to join me.

"Aren't you coming?"

Drake shakes his head. "I'd love to, but llamas don't feed themselves. I need to get them out of the barn and into the field. Besides, Henry will take good care of you."

"That's right." Henry spits the chewed-up piece of straw on the ground. "You visiting town?"

"I'm moving here," I answer.

The smile on Drake's face widens. "Now that is good news. I look forward to seeing you around, city girl. We can finish our—discussion another time."

"Our discussion?"

"The one in the barn." He gives me a wink.

I pray Henry doesn't notice the flush in my cheeks.

"Um, y-y-yes," I stammer, "that would be nice."

"Well, seeing how you're new," Henry says, completely missing the undercurrent of Drake's comments, "you'll probably want to stop in at Shelly's Diner after we get your car sorted. It's a great place if you're looking for home-cooked food. Taylor's grocery is the only place to grab your groceries, but it's closed on Sundays. If you're just wanting something quick, you can take a gander at Eddie's Soda Shoppe."

"Thank you," I say to Henry. "I'm new but not a stranger to Peace Springs. I spent my summers here as a girl."

"Really?" Drake's smile widens further.

"Yeah, but I haven't been here in about eight years."

"Well then," Drake says, scratching his chin. "Eddie's is still a great place. A lot of the kids hang out there. Though, if you're looking for quiet, you probably want to go to Shelly's Diner. I usually pop in there myself for Sunday dinners."

Is that an oblique invitation? Dinner will lead to an evening I want, but I'm not sure I should want it. Despite the ache from moments ago, I'm still worried about moving too fast.

As the new town doctor, I might need to rethink getting involved with the first man I meet. I can't help myself, though. Drake seems to have worked his way under my skin.

"I might just do that."

Uncle Pete probably has dinner plans, but I'll find a way to get out of them if it means spending the evening with Drake.

"Take care of my girl." Drake closes the distance with Henry, and the two men shake hands.

I climb into Henry's truck, disappointed Drake isn't able to come, but excited he wants to see me later.

The two men exchange a few words. It looks like Drake is giving directions, which is a good thing. I have no idea where my Jeep might be. Will we even be able to see it?

Henry joins me in the cab and cranks over the diesel engine. "Let's snag your car out of a ditch, pretty lady."

I rub my lips, remembering the press of Drake's mouth against mine. I wave to him as Henry pulls around. Drake stares back, the intensity of his gaze dangerous with the unspoken promise lingering between us.

10

PEONIES

TWO HOURS LATER, I PULL UP AT MY UNCLE'S HOUSE. HENRY WAS ABLE to drag my Jeep out of the ditch without a problem. He inspected my vehicle, checked the wheels, and made sure the rims weren't bent. The bumper needs to be replaced, but there isn't any other damage.

He stayed while I turned the motor over and had me pop the hood to make sure everything worked as it should. He even followed behind me, making sure I made it into town safe.

Henry refuses to charge me for the service, gives me a business card, and tells me to bring the car around when I want to get the bumper fixed. I give him a peck on the cheek and wave as he pulls away.

With a deep breath, I stare at my temporary home. Until I can find a place to live, Uncle Pete opened his house to me. It feels a little like coming home and finding a piece of my younger self.

I was always close to my aunt and uncle. My parents brought me here nearly every summer. It was something I looked forward to. Once school ended, there wasn't much for me to do in Redlands. I loved the small-town change of pace. It was so different from the crowded concrete jungle I grew up in. For that reason alone, Peace Springs always felt like a second home.

Now, I'll be calling it home for real. Although, it doesn't *feel* real yet.

There's a part of me that still believes this is temporary. Like when summer ends, I'll have to leave. After meeting Drake, Bert, and even Henry, I really want this to work.

Medical school and residency are behind me, but that doesn't mean I still don't have a lot to learn. Being a small-town doc is much harder than a family practice physician in a big city.

In Redlands, when I had a difficult case, it wasn't a problem referring my patients to see any number of different specialists. Not that I can't do that here, but instead of a ten-minute trip across town, my patients will be looking at upwards of a two-hour drive, and that's just to get to Billings.

All that's to say, I need to be on my A-game all the time. There's no room for error. At least, I'll have my uncle to lean on for a few years. By the time he's ready to retire, I should hit my stride.

So, I have a job, a place to live, and it looks like I have a romantic interest. Not to mention, I've met two incredibly helpful men. It feels as if everything is going better than planned.

Things couldn't be more perfect.

I tried calling my uncle on the way over, but he didn't pick up.

The country house lacks the white picket fence but it has a cobbled walk up to the door, a covered porch with the requisite porch swing, rocking chairs, and despite the snow covering the front lawn, the flower beds boast a riot of peonies in bloom. The doormat is one of those thick fiber mats. Instead of *Welcome,* it says, *Peace.*

I knock on the white-washed door of the little one-story home.

A tribute to the town perhaps, but Aunt Martha always said a home should not only welcome visitors but strive for peace and tranquility for those who live inside.

There's no answer at the door.

I knock harder and then peek through the windows.

Maybe he's out back, working in the shed?

I step off the porch and pick my way across the melting snow. The sun climbs high, and the temperature steadily rises from the chill of morning. At this rate, all the snow will be melted and gone within a day.

The door to the shed is locked. Uncle Pete always says a doctor needs a hobby, something to engage the creative side of the brain and give the scientific one a break. I have yet to find my creative side, too engaged with learning how to be the best doctor possible.

I miss sitting with him in the shed. He used to give me a blade and taught me to whittle. Never any good at it, all I ever managed was sharpening sticks, but it wasn't about making anything. It was all about hearing his stories. Because of his stories, I decided to pursue medicine.

My visits to Peace Springs stopped eight years ago when my focus shifted from kicking back to getting good grades and preparing for college. Little did I know that would be the year all our lives changed.

Uncle Pete diagnosed Aunt Martha's breast cancer that fall. Four years later, Aunt Martha lost her fight with cancer. My parents died in a car accident on the way to the funeral. Pete stayed in Peace Springs with his medical practice. I returned to Redlands to bury my parents and pick up the pieces of my life.

I haven't been back since. I regret that now.

Not much has changed in the town. My uncle's house looks the same as it did when Aunt Martha was alive.

I look forward to working with him and reconnecting. In his late fifties, he keeps talking about how much he looks forward to retiring and was thrilled when I pursued a family medicine residency because his dream was always to pass his practice on to his goddaughter.

Pete and Martha never had children of their own. They showered all their affections on their only niece, and I ate up the attention.

I walk to the back door, open the screen, and knock.

No answer.

It's Sunday.

He keeps crazy hours, makes house calls at all hours of the day, but he doesn't usually work on the day of the Lord, as Aunt Martha used to call it. I bang against the door and call out.

"Uncle Pete? Are you home?"

I should call again, but in the excitement of last night, I forgot to charge my phone. Henry was kind enough to let me borrow his, but I won't be calling anyone until mine's recharged. The poor thing was at five percent when my ordeal in the snow began. It's way past dead now and needs a deep recharge.

Where's my uncle?

Something acrid tickles my nostrils. A burning smell, not wood, floats on the air. Something pungent. And it's coming from inside.

I bang on the door, harder and more insistent this time.

Nothing.

Even though my aunt and uncle live in a small town, considered by many as one of the safest communities, Aunt Martha insisted on gardening for safety. That meant planting the thorniest bushes beneath every window to keep burglars out.

I climb over a holly bush, desperate to peek through the window because whatever is burning is coming from inside.

Barbs of pointed stems and holly leaves poke through my jeans and scratch my skin. I bite back a squeal as a thorny branch slices my upper arm.

The kitchen window perches a tad too high. I grip the windowsill and leverage myself up by bracing against the trunk of the offending bush. Branches break. I fall.

I scurry up again.

Peering into the house, thick black smoke curls up from a skillet on the stove. Bacon grease and the putrid smell of burned eggs creates the horrendous smell.

Where is Uncle Pete?

I twist left and right, trying to see inside.

There.

On the floor.

His feet poke out from the hallway.

I drop to the ground and race to the back door. My palm slams against the door.

"Uncle Pete!" My shrill cry rings out through the air.

The neighbor next door steps out onto her back porch. "What's all the hollering about?"

I recognize Mrs. Leesum and run to her. "Mrs. Leesum, it's me, Abigail Knight, Doctor Bateman's niece. Something's wrong. Can you call 9-1-1?"

"Is Doctor Bateman okay?" Mrs. Leesum's face pales, and I clutch at my chest.

"I don't know. Can you please call?"

Mrs. Leesum turns to duck back inside her house, but I call out. "Do you have a key?"

My aunt never believed in leaving a spare key outside. Too risky. Dangerous even. But maybe she gave a copy to the neighbors.

"Oh, yes," Mrs. Leesum says. "Let me grab it."

"Please, and then call 9-1-1."

Mrs. Leesum disappears inside and reappears a few moments later with a key in her hand and a cell phone pressed to her ear. I run back to the house as Mrs. Leesum speaks to whoever is on the other end of the line.

I shove the key in the lock. My pulse pounds with adrenaline, making my hands shake. It takes three tries before the lock turns. I barge in. My eyes cut to Uncle Pete's unmoving form. Acrid smoke fills the kitchen and burns my lungs.

Why didn't the fire alarms go off?

I turn off the gas to the stovetop and put a lid on the pan, then rush to my uncle. He lies face down on the floor. My fingers tremble as I feel for a pulse, terrified because I can't find one.

Where are the emergency response vehicles?

Then I pause, remembering who and what I am. I take a steadying breath. I'm trained for this.

I roll him over, placing him in the recovery position. I force my emotions to the background and focus on being the doctor I've trained to be.

Placing my fingers over his neck, I feel for his carotid pulse. Faint, but steady, his pulse thumps against my index finger. His chest moves with the slow rhythm of breathing.

So, why did he fall?

As far as I know, he isn't a diabetic. There's never been a reason for him to disclose his medical history, but low blood sugar is something I can fix. I leave him in the recovery position and rush to the kitchen.

Sugar. What kind of sugar does he have on hand?

Opening the fridge, I find what I need. Strawberry preserves. Perfect.

Returning to my uncle, I dip my finger in the jam, take a big scoop, and rub it inside his cheek. If his fall was the result of low blood sugar, that should raise it quickly enough.

Sirens sound. I run to the front door, unbolt the latch, and throw open the door. Walking onto the porch, I wave to the paramedics, urging them to move faster.

Two men jump out of the rig. One comes toward me, orange bag slung over his shoulder, while the other pulls a stretcher out of the back of the rig.

"Ma'am," the lead man says. "What's the problem?"

"It's my uncle. He passed out."

I follow him inside. "I gave him sugar, but I don't know what's wrong with him."

The man crouches beside my uncle and feels for a pulse. "Don't worry, ma'am, we'll take good care of the doc." He scrunches his eyes at me. "Hey, wait. You're Doctor Knight, aren't you?"

I nod. "That's me."

He breathes out a deep sigh. "Glad to meet you."

"You know me?"

He rolls up my uncle's sleeve and looks for a vein to place an IV. "Whole town has been waiting on you to arrive."

"You have?"

"Don't worry about Doc Bateman. He's given us instructions."

"Instructions?" What the hell is this guy talking about?

"We'll make sure he's comfortable. He's got a doctor in Billings and hospice has been arranged."

"What do you mean hospice?"

He pauses. "He didn't tell you?"

11

INHERITANCE

PANCREATIC CANCER.

Those two words fill my world with an ache so deep, I can't form a coherent thought.

The EMTs, Fred Cavanaugh and Tom Jenkins, allow me to ride in the ambulance for the two-hour ride to Billings. Tom works with a quiet efficiency, placing an IV into my uncle's hand and taping it securely in place. He hangs fluids, takes vitals, and scratches on a flowsheet.

"I'm sorry," he says after a prolonged silence. "You didn't know?"

I shake my head. "He didn't tell me."

Tom flicks his sandy blond bangs back from his freckled face and blows out a deep breath. "Well, it's not common knowledge. I don't think anyone really knows."

"You knew."

"Well, he had to tell us."

"How long?" How long has my uncle been dying? That's the question I want to ask. "When was he diagnosed?"

"A month or two at most. Maybe he was waiting to tell you in person?" Tom crinkles his nose, his brows pinching together.

"Maybe."

Would it change things? If I knew, would I have agreed to take over his practice one year out of residency? I planned on years, learning by his side. I'm not ready to practice alone.

The only reason I agreed was because I needed an excuse to leave Redlands. It was too easy to slip into an unhealthy relationship and even harder to leave it behind. My uncle gave me the perfect out because I sure as hell wasn't able to walk away on my own.

I wasted a year trying to establish myself as a new graduate, failing more often than not alongside a man who used his fists more than his heart.

My uncle's call saved my life, and the idea of working beside him fills me with pride. Never in a million years did I envision myself as a small-town doc, but he loves his job, and I've been excited to return to the town which filled my summers with love and cherished child-hood memories.

Now?

Pancreatic cancer?

All cancers are bad, but none sweep into a person's life with the same speed and devastation as pancreatic cancer.

There's palliative treatment, but no cure, and once diagnosed, the relentless course of the disease can rarely be slowed. Some people live a few years, but most die within months. If I understand what Tom says, my uncle only found out a couple of months ago.

We don't have enough time.

The ambulance races down the small highway and soon pulls up outside St. Vincent's emergency department in Billings.

"Thank you," I say my goodbyes to Tom and Fred.

"Our pleasure," Tom says. "Listen, if you need anything, give us a call. I'm sorry we had to meet under these circumstances. Doc Bateman says nothing but good things about you. I look forward to working with you."

Fred shakes my hand. "Seriously, anything you need, you call us."

A lump in my throat is the only thing holding back a flood of tears. I will soon be working with these men, and I don't want them to see me break down. Perhaps they understand because they don't pressure me for more conversation. They jump inside the ambulance and wave goodbye.

The staff of St. Vincent's places my uncle on the HemeOnc ward for observation overnight. The doctors tell me he's dehydrated and attributes his fall and subsequent disorientation to that, but they're thorough and examine him for any injury to his head from the fall. They fully expect a short stay and have hopes he might be released in the morning.

Visiting hours end, and I make reservations at a local motel. As I snuggle under the scratchy covers, my thoughts turn to the soft flannel of Bert's twin bed and to the magnanimous stranger who saved my life and kissed me senseless.

When I arrive at the hospital the next morning, Uncle Pete is sitting up in bed, picking at the food on his breakfast tray.

"Uncle Pete!" I race through the door and give him a hug.

He reaches up, returning a much weaker hug. "Abigail! Honey, it's so good to see you."

Leaning back, I look him over, unsure what to say. My eyes brim with tears and my heart aches. "I was so scared."

He bites at his lower lip. "They told me what happened." His shaky fingers brush back a lock of hair and his eyes pinch. "I'm sorry, hun. I wanted to tell you myself. I didn't expect ..."

"Tom told me."

Uncle Pete nods. "He's a smart kid, and dedicated." He pulls in a deep breath and blows it out in a rush.

"How advanced is it?"

He purses his lips. "Advanced enough."

"Tom mentioned hospice?"

"We're not quite there yet, but I expect it'll be soon."

I can't hold back the tears any longer.

"Hey," he says. "It's going to be okay."

"I just thought we'd have more time."

"I'm okay," he says. "I've found my peace, and Martha's been waiting long enough. It's time for me to join her."

He misses his wife. I can't fault him for that. Nearly eight years after my parents' deaths, the pain of their loss hits hard most days. He lost his wife, his soulmate, and maybe living without her hurts more than dying. At least he doesn't look scared confronting his death. Perhaps he truly is at peace with it, and if he is, then I will be too. Even if it makes my heart break.

"How was your drive?" he asks. "I thought you were supposed to get in last night?"

"I was."

"I worried about you on the roads and figured you'd stopped for the night."

I laugh. "Oh, Uncle Pete, do I have a story to tell you."

He scoots over, and I snuggle beside him. Telling him about my late-night adventures doesn't sound as scary in the comfort of his arms.

He gasps when I tell him about the moose and driving into the ditch. He barely believes me about the wolves or the overland hike. I don't get to tell him much about Drake because his team of doctors come in for rounds.

"Good news," Doctor Blount says. "We're cutting you loose."

"Oh, good," my uncle says. "I'm ready to go."

"We just have a bit of paperwork to take care of, and then you're cleared to go home."

When the team leaves, I kiss my uncle on the cheek. "Hey, I need to figure out how we're getting home." My Jeep is still sitting outside his house.

Briefly, I consider calling Tom, but he's probably working. Drake or Bert would be good choices, except I don't have either of their numbers. I thumb on my phone and search local car rentals. Hopefully, this won't hold up getting home.

After a bit of internet searching, I rent a car from a local rental agency. They make it easy and pick me up at the hospital. By the time I complete the required paperwork, my uncle is discharged. I meet him in his room and then walk with him while the nurse wheels him down to the hospital lobby. The whole way, I pay close attention to his balance, his stamina, everything really.

During the drive back, we talk about his wishes, both for end-of-life care and his funeral. The sobering discussion isn't easy, but he's thought about all the details. All I need to do is take care of a few loose ends.

"There's something else," he says.

"What's that?"

"It has to do with your inheritance."

"I don't need anything."

"I appreciate that, but this comes from your Aunt Martha's side of the family, and in many ways, from your mother as well."

"Really?"

An odd turn in the conversation, but I listen. I received a healthy inheritance from my parents. I invested most of the money in stocks, and the rest paid for medical school. I'm not rich, but I have comfortable reserves stashed away. Reserves that Scott thankfully never knew about. It never occurred to me to presume an inheritance from my aunt and uncle. It's one of those delicate topics not easily addressed.

"You're the last daughter in a long line of remarkable women."

I know a little of my family's legacy. One of my ancestors immigrated from Ireland during the potato blight, and after a few years, moved out west. I grew up with the stories about the women in my family making a home for themselves in the Wild West.

While he talks, I steal a glance at the odometer and try to gauge where I had my accident. I estimate I was five miles or less from town when I ran off the road.

My uncle coughs. "There's a trust which has passed from generation to generation. To avoid splitting the homestead, it passed through the firstborn daughters. Since Martha and I never had children, she intended for you to inherit the trust. On your thirtieth birthday, you'll gain control."

"What are you talking about? What homestead?"

He tugs on the shoulder strap of his seat belt and shifts to a more comfortable position. "You've been there. Martha and your mom took you when you came to visit."

I remember trips out of town. Long drives and even longer days playing in the eddies of a slow-moving river, learning to skip stones and fly fish. It never occurred to me to ask about who owned the land.

"We had fun. I remember hot summer days, swimming, and hiking. Mom would build a fire, and Aunt Martha brought stuff to make s'mores. We stayed past dark and watched shooting stars."

"That's the place."

"It would be fun to go back and explore."

He coughs again. "There's a lot to explore."

"Do you think there's enough space to build?" My childhood memories include a longish ride in the back of a car, but I can't remember how far from town the land might be.

"Abby," he says, his voice turning serious. "I don't think you understand."

"Understand, what?"

"It's more than a place to plop a house."

"Well, a few acres will be harder to maintain, but I'm sure I can handle it."

He laughs. "Honey, the parcel is over ten thousand acres. You're a landowner now, and there are things you need to know about that land."

"Excuse me?"

12

CHOCOLATE CHIP PANCAKES

BACK AT UNCLE PETE'S HOUSE, I MAKE SURE HE'S COMFORTABLE AND then clean the mess in the kitchen. The pan goes into the garbage. There's no way to salvage it. I'll buy him a new one later.

A glance around the house eases my mind. I equate cancer with disability, and assume my uncle fell behind in his chores, but there isn't any reason to be worried.

What concerns me is why he passed out. I have a feeling he's sicker than he's letting on. He lost a lot of weight, and that worries me more than anything else.

I put a cartridge in the coffee maker and grab two mugs from the cupboard. Like me, he takes his coffee black. It's a much easier and cheaper alternative for those used to long days and even longer nights on call.

"Here you go." I hand him his cup and settle on the couch, tucking my legs beneath me. "Is there anything you need me to do work-wise?" Being that it's Monday, I worry about any patients scheduled to see him.

He waves off my questions. "Don't worry, Angie will see to the appointments. She's the receptionist."

"What about the urgent care patients? If you're not there, where do they go?"

"A lot of urgent visits aren't that urgent at all. I have two nurse practitioners who help run urgent care."

"Well," I say. "I can see them if you want."

We discussed giving me a couple of weeks to get settled after my move, but I prefer staying busy. The sum total of my possessions is packed inside three suitcases.

"If you're feeling up to it, I'd like to check out the clinic."

He smiles. "I'm happy you decided to take a chance on Peace Springs." Rising from his chair, he gathers my empty coffee cup. "I think you're going to find it's a great place to live. Let me shower, and I'll introduce you to the clinic staff."

"I think I'm the one who needs to get cleaned up." I'm still wearing the same clothes from my accident. "I'm going to get my things from outside. Am I staying in the library?"

During my summer visits, my aunt and uncle put me in the library. They have a Murphy bed I thought was cool as a kid, but as an adult, I'm not excited to sleep on the overly firm mattress.

"No, hun, the guest room is yours." That's the room my parents stayed in.

"Thanks."

"Do you need help with your bags?"

The thought of him carrying the heavy luggage makes me pause, but he doesn't want to be treated any differently.

"Um, yeah. Thanks."

I give him the dilapidated fern and the smaller suitcase. Time will tell about Boston, but it doesn't look like the freezing temperatures killed it. At least not yet. A few minutes later, we have my bags in the guest room. It's almost eleven.

"Let me change, and maybe we can grab lunch before we head to the clinic?" I suggest.

"Sounds like a plan." He glances around the room. "You know where everything is. Towels, soap, and shampoo are in the bathroom closet."

"I got it. You take a shower and freshen up. We'll make it a day on the town."

A crooked smile lights up his face. "You have a hankering for milkshakes?"

I shake my head. "Actually, I was thinking of hitting up Shelly's Diner."

"Ah, yes, best pancakes in town. It'll be lunchtime, but I bet we can convince her to whip some up."

"Chocolate chips?"

"I delivered all of Shelly's kids. I can talk her into a few chocolate chip pancakes."

I would prefer the shake. As a kid, I begged to go to Eddie's retro-themed soda shoppe almost every day. Maybe it's silly heading to Shelly's and foolish to think I'll run into Drake. Maybe I confused that kiss for something more. But I want to know if that kiss was all in my head.

There are a lot of maybes in my life, but one thing is certain. I need a shower.

It takes a little digging to find my makeup. Normally, I wouldn't bother, but this is my first time meeting the clinic staff. I want to make a good first impression, especially since I'll soon be their boss. What I really wish is that I had Drake's number.

Wait.

Henry gave me his card. My car needs repairs, and Henry knows Drake. Maybe I can work around to a reintroduction to Drake.

My uncle waits in the living room when I finally emerge. My long hair is pulled back into a ponytail. I don't like how it accentuates the angles of my face or draws attention to what I consider to be overly large green eyes. Given a choice, I prefer my hair loose, but I don't have time to dry it. I'm eager to poke around town, not to mention I'm starving.

"You ready?" My uncle dresses for comfort, jeans and a button-down shirt.

I prefer jeans, but dress in black slacks and a pale-yellow blouse, professional, but not stuffy. "You clean up well," I tease.

We pile into my Jeep and head into town. During the drive, child-hood memories bubble to the surface, hitting me, not in the gut, but in my heart.

When I came to Peace Springs, I envied the children who grew up together in grade school, still knew each other through junior high, and matured into adults in high school. The kids were friendly, but I was always an outsider. Despite that, Peace Springs feels comfortable.

Not home yet, but maybe someday soon.

I turn the Jeep onto Main Street

It doesn't take long to drive through town. Nor is it difficult to find a parking spot. I pull up right outside Shelly's Diner. I walk into the busy diner and inhale the mouthwatering aromas coming from the open kitchen. The clinking of silverware and glass slows somewhat as Uncle Pete enters. Several people give him a nod, a polite acknowl-edgment of respect.

He guides me to an empty booth by the window. When our wait-ress arrives, he orders two short stacks with chocolate chips and a pot of coffee. The girl doesn't bat an eye, making me think his order isn't as unusual as I think.

"It looks exactly like I remember." I lean back and peer out the window.

"Not much changes here. Of course, there's town politics and such, the never-ending feud, the occasional scandal, who's sleeping with whom. You're going to learn way more than you ever wanted about the residents. People in this town seem to think their doctor is a stand-in for their confessional."

"Really?"

We talk about his practice, touching on the business aspects, but when our food arrives, I broach something that is bugging me.

"Uncle Pete," I begin, "how did Aunt Martha get ten thousand acres?" More importantly, how will I manage a ranch that size? The real estate taxes are going to be fierce.

"Accumulated through the generations," he says. "As a matter of fact, it is your namesake who homesteaded the very first parcel." His eyes brighten. "Oh, and you're in for a treat."

"How's that?"

He takes in a deep breath. "Well, Abigale McPhearson's journal is waiting for you. I don't know how much your mother told you, but Abigale immigrated to the United States during the great potato blight in Ireland when she was a teenager."

"I remember a little bit about that." I take a sip of the dark-roast coffee, closing my eyes at the decadent flavor. "I couldn't imagine picking up your whole life and leaving everything behind."

He laughs.

"What's so funny?"

"Says the woman whose entire life is packed into three suitcases."

I roll my eyes. "Tell me about my great-great-great- whatever grandmother."

"I'll do better than that. Remind me when we get home, and I'll give you the journal."

"A journal? Wow, thanks. What's in it?"

He shrugs. "I have no idea. Martha says it is a McPhearson-women-eyes-only kind of thing." He shoves a bite of pancake into his mouth and wipes his chin with a napkin. "Abigale was the first to settle down here. Back then, women weren't allowed to own land in most states, but Montana has always been progressive. As long as someone was the head of household, they could apply for a home-stead. She moved out west and put down roots. Her daughter and her daughter's twins homesteaded as well, doubling the size of the home-stead parcels."

"Twins?" I know little about my family's history.

He nods. "Yes, can you imagine delivering twins in the late 1800s?" He pushes his food around his plate, his appetite seems to have disappeared. "Anyway, they added to the homestead and later filed the deeds to own the land. They raised cattle and bought up the surrounding homesteads as they were abandoned. Soon, they turned a thousand acres into two, and then more. Every generation continued the tradition. The land went into trust somewhere along the way. It can't be broken down and sold off. It was one of Abigale's wishes for the land to stay in the family. Martha mentioned something about it being spelled out in the diary."

"How am I going to manage ten thousand acres?"

"The arable plots are leased out to farmers who grow feed for cattle. Cattle ranchers lease out the pastureland for grazing. It's practically self-sustaining and makes more than enough to pay the taxes. As far as managing it, there's a manager who takes care of all that."

"Well, if it's supposed to stay in the family, I won't sell it."

Ten thousand acres? What the hell am I going to do with that?

13

PORCH SWING

W<small>E</small> <small>SPEND THE AFTERNOON AT THE CLINIC WHERE</small> U<small>NCLE</small> P<small>ETE</small>
introduces me to the staff. He fatigues as the afternoon wears on and
I soon take him home, concerned by his lack of stamina.

He doesn't talk any more about the trust, or my inheritance,
except to say he scheduled a meeting with his lawyer. He brings
Abigale McPhearson's leather journal out, presenting it to me with
reverence, then excuses himself for the night.

Over a hundred years old, the journal's weathered the decades
with amazing grace. The pages are yellowed with age but remain
supple, not cracking as I would expect.

He says the contents are meant for McPhearson women's eyes
only, but I wonder if he ever stole a peek through the years. Knowing
my uncle's character, he probably never considered it, respecting the
family tradition.

I settle in Aunt Martha's recliner, excited to read my namesake's
words. The first pages include a family tree and the passing of the
journal through the first-born daughters. Aunt Martha's name is the
last entry with a penned line for the first-born daughter she
never had.

I rub my finger over that empty space. My name goes there, but how to annotate it correctly? Then it hits me. I'm the last female in the McPhearson line. Before I finish tracing Martha's lineage back through the decades, a knock sounds at the front door.

"Coming," I call out.

Opening the door, my breath catches. Drake stands, hand raised, ready to knock on the door again.

"Drake?" The quickening of my pulse catches me off guard. There's just so much of *him* to take in. From the devastation of his dark eyes to the jagged scar on his cheek, he quickens my breath and brings heat to my face.

Incredibly handsome, Drake stands with purpose, his feet spread on a wide base, completely unaware of how his overwhelming presence makes my heart flutter.

A storm brews in his eyes, not of anger, but of a more pressing need. Cotton strains over the broad expanse of his chest, every ripple of muscle outlined underneath. With his height, my attention focuses firmly on the cut definition of his chest and the bulge of his biceps. I catch myself staring and drag my attention up to take in the rugged features of his face.

He crooks up a dark eyebrow, fully aware I'm checking him out. Heat builds in my cheeks, and the curve of his lips bows into a grin.

"City girl," he says with a mischievous smirk. "Bert told me I could find you at Doc Bateman's house. I've never been stood up by a girl before, must be something you city folk do all the time. You owe me a dinner date."

"I'm sorry. Something came up."

The breeze blowing in through the doorway is warm. The unseasonably cold weather seems to be on its way out.

"I was just ..."

"You were *just* getting ready to tell me how you're going to make it up to me." He palms the door jamb and dares me to deny his demand.

Speechless, my ribs expand with a sharp inhale while I stare at him like a fool.

A devilish grin takes control of his face, softening the jagged line of his scar. The stubble across his hard jaw makes me itch to run my fingers across the coarse whiskers and steal another taste of him. We regard each other for a minute until he leans in to whisper in my ear.

"I'm reading your mind, and while I'd love to take another kiss, let me take you on a proper date first."

My breath rushes out as the whisper-light press of his lips against the side of my neck makes my muscles tense and my heart race. My fingernails bite into my palms with the struggle to not lose all control.

He lets out a strained laugh, his lips hovering over my ear again. "An odd thing we've got going, isn't it?"

"Yes." My voice wavers with my response. "What is it?"

"The air crackles between us. Tell me you're interested in exploring this further."

Interested?

That word doesn't begin to describe the need burning within me, but I didn't leave a bad relationship to jump blindly into another. And I'm certainly not ready to land in any man's bed after knowing him for only one night, even if he saved my life.

I step back, breaking the electrical connection supercharging the air. I need a breath without his overwhelming *Drake-ness* muddling my thoughts.

"Um, give me a second." I bite down on my cheek.

The polite thing would be to invite him in, but I have a feeling things will rapidly escalate if we're in a room alone together. When Drake doesn't budge, I make a big deal of closing the door. If he wants to play the city-country angle, then he can wait on the porch like a proper country gentleman.

As soon as I shut the door, I bring my hands to my mouth to suppress a girly squeal, then I press my shoulders back, and try to gain some semblance of control. He tracked me down the same way I planned on finding him.

I run to my room and rummage through my suitcases until I find a black skirt. The fabric doesn't need ironing and is perfect for an emergency outfit change. Shimmying out of my pants, I pull on the skirt, hoping Drake will appreciate the tight fit.

Since it is still cool outside, I opt for a dark sweater and layer a dressy tank top underneath. I have no idea what he intends—there are few bars in Peace Springs—but if they're anything like the ones in Redlands, a sweater will be too hot if there's a crowd heating up the inside.

I grab my purse and drape the coat Bert lent me over my arm. I want Drake to get the full impact of my outfit and will endure the discomfort of the chilly night air.

A quick peek at the mirror beside the front door, and I take in a deep breath. My uncle's in bed, and while I don't want to leave without letting him know I'm going out, I don't want to disturb him either. Instead, I scratch out a note and leave it on the door of the fridge.

Whatever happens with Drake tonight, I'll approach it with an open mind. One-night stands aren't my thing, but maybe it will do some good to put my ex firmly in the past.

When I step out onto the porch, Drake sits on the porch swing. His long legs rock him forward and back. He stills, and his eyes latch on to me. I shut the door quietly, taking care not to wake my uncle.

"Holy hell," Drake says.

"What's wrong?"

Between one breath and the next, he closes the distance and presses me against the door.

There is no preamble. No slow exhale as our lips wait to meet. Aggressive and powerful, he leans against me, the weight of his body blanketing me with his commanding presence. He wraps an arm around my waist, claiming me with his strength as his powerful lips take my mouth prisoner.

I wrap my hands around his neck and surrender to the kiss. My rational mind tells me to think this through. It's too fast. Too soon. I need to get settled before attaching myself to a man, or worse, sleeping with a stranger.

What will the town think of their new doctor? But my heart refuses to listen and chases those thoughts aside. For now, I'm willing to live on the edge and deal with the consequences later.

He flattens his palm against the small of my back, and the kiss softens with the kneading of his fingertips against my spine.

A lick.

A nip.

A final press of his lips and he breaks off the kiss.

With his forehead pressed against mine, we share an intimate moment. His breath spills out and swirls into my lungs. His scent, a mixture of wood smoke, earth, and musk, makes my eyes close and my head tip back against the door. He follows me, pressing his forehead to mine, keeping our connection intact.

"What the hell," he says with a weighted sigh. "Please tell me something really important came up and that's why I didn't see you at Shelly's."

My eyes drift shut. The press of his lips fade from my mouth, but the taste of him lingers, making me need more. Slowly, I open my eyes. Hardly any distance separates us, and while I can't focus on his eyes, I don't need to see them to feel the darkness swirling inside.

"Something came up. I'm sorry I didn't call, but I didn't have your number."

"Where is it?"

"Where's, what?"

He thrusts out his hand. "Your phone. Where is it?"

"In my purse."

"Give it to me," he demands.

"Why?"

"Because you need my number."

I undo the clasp of my purse and fish out my phone. Unlocking the screen, I dutifully hand it over. With a few quick taps, he enters his number and hands the phone back.

"There, now no more excuses for not calling."

The bossiness of his tone takes me back. Scott was nearly as pushy. It started with one demand, followed by another. When I made a mistake, his disappointment flared. Within a month of moving in together, he hit me the first time.

Drake only asks for my phone, but it makes me cautious.

I duck out from beneath him, surprising myself nearly as much as him. The sizzling energy which charges the air fizzles and dies.

"Um, maybe we should slow down a bit?"

His eyes pinch. "Did I do something wrong?"

Yes and no, but how to explain that without exposing the details of an abusive past?

"No." It isn't a complete lie, but neither is it the truth. "It's just, being new, I don't want people to get the wrong idea ..."

"Meaning you don't want me to get the wrong idea." He brushes aside the fringe of his dark bangs and straightens to his full height.

I place my palm against his chest. Warmth pulses from him to my fingertips, our connection strong enough to travel up my arm and swirl around my heart. Hesitant not to ruin the evening before it even begins, I bite at my lower lip.

"That kiss was ..."

"Hot," he says with a smirk.

I place my hands on his shoulders and balance on tiptoe until I can brush my lips against his. "It was amazing, but faster than I'm used to."

Socially reserved, it generally takes me forever to warm up to anyone. It took five dates before I let Scott kiss me the first time, and I didn't sleep with him for months after we started dating.

If Henry hadn't arrived with his tow truck and interrupted what was happening in that barn, I'm certain Drake would've followed through on his promise.

And the strangest thing?

I want to know how it feels to be led by nothing other than the flames of passion because I never allow myself the freedom to find out.

His finger lifts my chin and forces me to look him in the eyes. "I swear, city girl, sometimes I can see your mind churning its gears." He grips my hand and gives it a squeeze. "Now, how about we see to dinner? Maybe hit a bar? Monday nights, there's not much happening around here, but we can find a bar with a jukebox, and I bet I can clear the floor and take you for a twirl."

Dancing?

Oh no! Anything but that.

"How about dinner and a couple of drinks? We can leave the dancing to the kids."

He wraps his hands around my waist, picks me up, and twirls me in the air. "Fuck that, you're dancing with me."

I squeal as he spins me around. When he stops, a banked heat smolders in his eyes. At first, I stare down at him, and then he lowers me slowly.

Our eyes meet.

He presses his lips against mine, this time giving a slow, gentle caress. Then he lowers me still until I have to crane my neck.

A breath in, and his dark, heady musk fills my nasal passages. My feet have yet to reach the ground, but I don't care. I never care if I ever walk again.

Laying my cheek against the expanse of his chest, I breathe out a sigh, feeling content for the first time in years.

"No dancing," I say.

"You let me decide." He places a kiss on my forehead. "I won't steer you wrong."

14

KING RANCH

* * *

A SMALL TOWN OF A FEW THOUSAND, PEACE SPRINGS BARELY SUPPORTS the need for a doctor. Which means, there isn't much to do in town on a Monday night.

"What do you have in mind for dinner?" I'm interested to find out what constitutes a good time in such a small town.

While growing up, my visits here were the adventures of a child. A night on the town included a burger, a shake at Eddie's Soda Shoppe, and being allowed to stay out past nine.

He holds my hand, supporting me as I take the steps leading off the porch. Sitting beside my Jeep, a black F250 heavy duty King Ranch chirps and flashes its lights.

"It's a surprise," he answers with a wink. "I'm thinking something special for a city girl."

"I wish you'd stop calling me that." Except, I love the way the words roll off his tongue and how his eyes simmer when he says them.

"I could call you *pumpkin?*"

"Pumpkin!" I turn to face him. "You're not serious?"

"Well, if I have to pick something else, that's what I'm going with."

"How about Abby? It *is* my name."

His head tilts to the side, and he pulls at his chin. "Everyone else will be calling you that. I want something that's all mine." He shrugs. "Your pick, *pumpkin* or *city girl?*"

"I'm not a pumpkin."

"I agree. You taste sweeter than a pumpkin."

"You haven't answered my question." I turn away, not wanting him to see me blush.

"About where we're going?"

"Yes."

"Because I'm planning on surprising you."

Well, it isn't going to be much of a surprise. There are really only two places to eat and a handful of bars.

He won't take me to Bar 21. It caters to a seedier crowd, which leaves Top Bar as the only other option. The only one I know that has music and anything resembling a dance floor is Top Bar.

My father took me there a few times after work when he wanted to relax with a beer. First, he would grab me a shake at Eddie's. Then I spent the afternoon reading or coloring, sipping my milkshake, while he talked with the men.

"There aren't that many places to go."

"How much do you trust me?"

That answer is way more complicated than it should be.

We reach his truck and, when he opens the passenger door, a length of black silk drapes across the seat.

"What's that for?" I claim to be open-minded, but when it comes to kinky sex games, I'm as vanilla as they come. Not to mention we barely know each other.

He laughs as I back away, but he stops me with the brace of his arm.

Reaching over my shoulder, he grabs the silky fabric. "It's a blind-fold, silly." He gives another of his knee-knocking winks. "Let's get beyond the first kiss or two before we spice things up by tying you up."

My mouth gapes and heat rises to my cheeks. "That's not what I meant."

"Oh, if you could see the color of your cheeks. Hell, instead of pumpkin, I should've gone with *sugar beet.* Now those are sweet and beet red."

I punch him playfully in the arm and shake out my fist. "Ow!"

"Hey, don't be hollering at me. You punched me." Drake laughs. "I'm not planning on tying you up. It's just a blindfold. I have something special planned, and I don't want to spoil it."

I slow my breathing and blush again. This time for letting his teasing get under my skin.

"Promise you'll stop making fun of me?"

"Sorry, but I can't make a promise I know I won't keep." He lifts the silky fabric. "Now, do you trust me enough to play along?"

Trust shouldn't be such a complicated thing, but I hesitate. The look on his face is what finally has me saying yes. There's no malice in his expression. Instead, a desperate hope hungers in his gaze.

He saved me from wolves. Force marched me through the cold. I've gone over and over those few hours—how he refused to slow the pace and barely helped me through the worst spots. He did it on purpose to ensure I kept my body temperature up by keeping me moving.

The moment I was out of danger, he's been nothing but gentle. Teasing me more often than not, but he's never been gruff, and certainly not disinterested.

Scott and his physical abuse traumatized me, but I refuse to let him influence how I respond to every other man in my life.

"I trust you."

"Good." He twirls his finger in the air.

I dutifully spin and face away from him.

His strong fingers place the fabric over my eyes. The touch ignites a banked heat slumbering in my core, making me gasp.

"Here, hold this while I tie you up."

I hold the silk in place and laugh. "You said no tying me up."

"Well, not yet, but I have to warn you, I'm a rancher."

"And?"

"I'm good with rope."

"A llama rancher. I know."

"Bert raises llamas. I run cattle, which means I'm really good with rope."

"Oh!" My insides squirm with the promise laced in his words.

Vanilla is good, but maybe a few chocolate sprinkles might be nice from time to time. While I focus on soothing my racing heart, his deft fingers tie the blindfold in place. He grips my shoulders and spins me around.

"Can you see anything?"

"Nope."

"You peeking?"

"No," I say with a laugh. "I'm not peeking. I can't see anything."

"Good."

The moment the word's out of his mouth, the searing heat of his kiss returns, all the hotter for how unexpected it is. I gasp. Then he lifts me up and settles me on the seat of the truck.

"Can you buckle in on your own, or do you need help?" He hands me the shoulder strap, and I feel at my left hip for the seatbelt latch.

"I've got it."

"Good, buckle up, city girl. I've got a treat for you."

The door shuts with a solid thunk, and I hear nothing but his boots on the ground as he rounds the truck. The driver's door opens, and the truck shifts under his weight.

"You a country, pop, or hard rock kind of gal?"

I take in a deep breath. "Your choice. I like them all."

The engine cranks over and classical music spills from the radio.

"Is that what you like?" I ask.

"Depends on my mood. I'm kind of in a Disturbed state of mind. Do you mind?"

I pause and then smile when I realize he means the rock group. "I love Disturbed."

"Well, settle in and get comfortable. Tell me if the music gets too loud." He cranks the sound as the first notes of a new song race out of the speakers.

Conversation comes to an end with the full-bodied sound, leaving me to wonder if Drake is headbanging or banging his hand on the steering wheel.

Either way, the music allows me to sink into my thoughts. And while his woodsy scent permeates the cab of the truck, at least I'm not subjected to his primal beauty during the drive.

I need time alone with my thoughts and to prepare for what might come next. I'm equally terrified of moving too slow as I am of moving too fast.

Keeping track of where he's driving proves impossible, although I try. My memory of Peace Springs is that of a kid riding a bicycle.

I follow the drive down the lane from my uncle's house, the turn left, which brings us past the elementary school. The rough road smooths out, telling me we've reached the center of town, but that's as far as my misguided directional sense goes.

"Where are you taking me?"

"What part of surprise do you not understand?"

"Just wondering how long we're going to be driving around. Surely we're on Main Street by now."

He huffs a laugh. "Just sit back and enjoy the ride. We'll get there when we get there."

Is he deliberately trying to get me lost?

I tap the armrest, my fingers drumming out my frustration. When I lift my hand to yank the blindfold off, his fingers curl around my wrist, tugging it down.

"Uh-uh, city girl. Just a bit longer and we'll be there."

"Where?"

"Dinner and dancing, of course."

Ugh. Maybe they built someplace new in town? It makes sense. A lot of small towns expand their borders by incorporating surrounding lands. Old farms are taken over and barns get turned into dance halls. Maybe that's what he has in mind?

Sure feels that way.

The truck moves from the easy ride over asphalt to a bumpier ride over an unpaved road. Rock and gravel grind beneath the tires, which means we moved onto one of the many unimproved roads surrounding town. A few minutes turn to ten, and then a few more.

"Almost there," he says. "Promise you'll sit tight for a second? I need to open the gate."

Open the gate? Must be a renovated farm. This town has more head of cattle than it does people. Cattle gates are as ubiquitous as blades of grass in the fields.

"I promise." And while the temptation to peek is overpowering, I don't want to ruin his surprise. Not after he went to so much trouble.

The driver's side door opens and the truck rocks as he exits. When he returns, he settles into his seat and grips my hand.

"Tell me," he says, "favorite movie genre."

"Um, I don't know."

The one thing about medical school, and the even more rigorous residency training, is a distinct lack of free time. I can't remember the last time I watched a movie, let alone saw one in a movie theater.

"I like a good science fiction piece."

"*Star Wars* geek or Trekkie?"

"Both I guess." Both franchises released movies recently. I'm not a complete mushroom and do manage to see some movies when they come out online. "I like the one with the mutants too."

"Ah, great. Perfect even." His long fingers stroke the back of my hand. "Do you have to be anywhere tomorrow? Need to check in with work?"

"Not yet. I'm still settling in." Not a complete lie, but the medical practice can wait another day.

"Good," he whispers. "I plan to have you out all night."

All night? My stomach flutters with what that might entail.

15

MAIN FEATURE

I NEVER THOUGHT A BLINDFOLD COULD BE COMFORTABLE. BUT IT IS. THE silk rests softly over my eyes.

Drake helps me out of the truck, using the maneuver to sneak in another kiss.

Hot, molten, sexy as sin, his lips capture mine, worshiping me as his expert tongue does things I never dreamed possible.

I ache for him.

After a simple kiss?

How is that possible?

Scott never made me feel this way. Hell, I never made myself feel this way when frustration drove me to take care of things myself.

I surrender beneath the quickening rush of his exhales feathering against my skin. He moves from my mouth to my neck, teasing and tickling, as he works up to suck on my earlobe where that talented tongue turns me into a quivering mess.

His low, throaty chuckle tells me two things. First, he's having fun with me. Second, he's a masterful kisser and knows it.

His confidence is dreamy. In his hands, beneath the expert torture of his tongue, I can lower my defenses and do something I've never done before.

I can be soft, willing, and captivated. I can blissfully surrender, letting him take the lead. There's no thought about the physical act to come. Instead of enduring sex, I luxuriate in the gentle nibbles and kisses, licks and nips Drake is intent on delivering.

He moves from my earlobe back down the sensitive skin of my neck, making me burn beneath the heat of his kiss. The man is one hundred percent focused on my pleasure. Yet another thing I'm not accustomed to.

I moan as his hand wraps in the hair at my nape, gripping and pulling with intent. Drake's certainly a take-charge kind of man, and right about now, he could ask me to do anything, and I'd say yes.

Dear Lord, when did I start trembling? When did I start making those delirious moans? He turns me into a wanton creature, and I've never been that. I've never not been in control.

My skin burns beneath the heat of his mouth, then shivers as he moves on to stimulate and torture the next square inch. I can barely think, but there's one thing I want.

"When are you going to let me remove the blindfold?" I ask, after catching my breath from his kiss.

"Soon, city girl." He whispers the endearment into my ear, nuzzling my neck before grasping my hand and leading me forward. "The ground is a bit uneven, but you should be okay."

"I'm not going to trip, am I?"

"If you do, I'll catch you."

I believe him.

A part of me wonders if he'll always be there to catch me when I fall—both in the literal sense and the figurative. That's another thing I've never had.

I've never been able to lean on anyone else. Scott called it *needy* when I asked for his help and was always put out of his way to assist me with whatever problem I was having.

Drake's already gone above and beyond.

His kisses move from my throat to meander along my collar bone. He ends his exploration at the tip of my shoulders.

"You're tickling me." I wriggle in his arms.

"Get used to it, luv. I'm going to be doing a whole lot more soon enough."

I've lost count of the number of moans spilling from my mouth.

We aren't in town. Or, if we are, we aren't on Main Street. The ground beneath my feet is uneven and crunches with dirt and gravel. Maybe my thoughts about a renovated barn aren't that far off base.

But he wouldn't kiss me like this in a parking lot. Drake doesn't seem to be that kind of man who would maul his blindfolded date where others can see.

So, where are we?

His fingers tighten as he guides me over the uneven ground, telegraphing his excitement. My skin shivers with the absence of the heat from his mouth.

"Almost there." He pulls up short and releases my hand. "Don't move."

The air holds an earthy scent, full of loam, dirt, pine, and wood smoke.

A fire?

The crackling of wood drifts to my ears. The aromatic smell of wood smoke brings back memories of the summers I spent in Peace Springs as a girl. I love camping out, staying up late, watching the stars overhead, and wishing time would stand still so that it would never end.

Gravel crunches under Drake's boots and another set of footsteps joins his. I lift my hands to the blindfold, curious as to who else is here, but stop. Keeping the blindfold in place seems important to Drake. I don't want to ruin whatever surprise he has planned.

Low tones of a conversation drift to my ears. Male voices. The deep rumble of Drake's and another, vaguely familiar, voice.

"Thanks," Drake says.

"No problem. Have fun."

Is that Bert?

Crickets chirp all around me. Cicadas fill the background with a droning noise. The gentle calls of songbirds roosting for the night complete the evening melody.

A light gusting of the wind brings other scents to my nose, deeper pungent aromas of animals and the sizzling of—steak?

The deep throaty rumble of a diesel truck sounds. Tires crunch over gravel and fade away.

Drake returns. "You doing okay?"

"You've got my attention," I say. "Was that Bert?"

He snickers. "Yeah, I asked him to get a few things set up."

The clatter of a generator sputters and hums. The only reason I have any familiarity with that sound is from my summer camping trips. My uncle always had a generator on hand, especially in the heat of the summer.

While we roughed it on the land, our tents were cooled by portable air conditioning units at night. There is roughing it and *roughing it*.

"Please," I beg. "Can I take the blindfold off?"

It's killing me wondering what Drake is up to.

He has a way of filling up space, even when I can't see him. His palpable presence tingles along my skin and hitches my breath. He's in every inhale and each beat of my heart, enveloping me in a world of what-ifs and what may be.

He cups my cheek. "God, you're beautiful." His fingers trace a path over my skin, skimming over my lips.

Compliments make me self-conscious, and I turn away. "Drake ..."

The heat of his lips brushes over my mouth. "You're amazing." His fingers slide under the silk at my temples. "Keep your eyes closed. I'm going to remove the blindfold, but don't look just yet."

"Okay." I press my hands against the hard ridge of his abdomen, drop them to my sides where I fiddle with the hem of my skirt. The overwhelming nearness of him makes my knees weak and my legs unsteady.

The silk lifts.

Strong hands grip my shoulders, and Drake spins me to face the other way.

"You ready?"

"As I'll ever be," I say.

The tip of his nose presses against the side of my neck. "Open your eyes, city girl."

I blink to clear my vision. A firepit crackles with burning wood. Two wooden chairs stand before it. A generator hums somewhere off to my left, black electrical wires snake to a table placed on the far side of the fire where a projector flickers in the waning light of dusk.

Strung between two massive oak trees, a white sheet stretches between the branches. Rope passes through corner grommets and loops around the branches, pulling the fabric taut. The lower corners are fixed in place, tied to two large rocks.

"A movie screen?"

A *Star Wars* movie trailer scrolls across the makeshift screen.

"I thought a night at the movies would be a treat. The drive-in isn't open during the week."

"So, you made one?"

My mouth waters with the aroma of whatever is cooking on that grill. I approach the firepit, leaving Drake where he is.

"What is this?"

"Well, my first thought was to cook steak. But it's a bit of a production."

Four skewers of meat are propped over the fire. Drops of fat and other juices fall from the meat to sizzle in the fire below.

I spin around. "I can't believe you did all of this."

"I'm full of surprises."

"Well, this is one hell of a surprise." I point to the screen. "I love *Star Wars*."

"Awesome. I've got all of them loaded up and ready to play."

"All of them?"

"Yup," he says. "All of them. You did say you didn't have anywhere to be in the morning."

I did at that.

The sun dips below the rim of the valley walls and the temperature drops.

Dusk ushers in the coming of night, and as the day fades, the sky blossoms with one of the most remarkable sunsets I've ever seen.

"This is simply amazing." I twirl in a circle, trying to soak it all in. "What a perfect place for a first date."

"I'm glad you approve, and a first date means there will be many more. I consider tonight a roaring success already." His grin is simply stunning, even with the scar.

Once we know each other better, I'm going to ask about that scar. For now, it doesn't matter. I'm officially head over heels, entranced by the man standing before me.

"We're going to have to wait until it gets a little darker before we can see the movie screen."

I glance at the screen and the faded image of a battle in the stars. I feel like I need to pinch myself because none of this can be real. Instead, I breathe in the crisp night air, drawing the wonderful aromas deep into my lungs. "What happens if I get cold?"

"We snuggle." The corner of his mouth turns up.

Snuggling sounds like fun.

16

SNUGGLING

THE LONG LOWING OF A COW BREAKS THE SILENCE. I TURN TOWARD THE
setting sun and look upon a group of cattle who graze near the fence-
line some distance away.

"Do you think they know what we're grilling?"

He laughs. "Let's hope not. I don't want them giving me the eye all
night long."

"Well, it looks wonderful. Smells amazing. And I can't wait for our
feature to begin. You'll rewind to the beginning once it's dark?"

"Absolutely."

"I really love this place."

"Do you?"

"Yes. Open sky. Rolling hills. I loved coming here as a kid. It
always felt so relaxed compared to home."

"It's definitely not full of people. I guarantee we're the only
humans within fifty acres."

"Do you have something against people?"

There's no sign of a tent. Other than the fire, the chairs, the generator, and screen it doesn't look as if he intends to spend the night.
And that's when I realize all the snow from the blizzard is gone.

Green grass waves in the evening breeze.

"What's wrong?" he asks.

"The snow. What happened to it?"

"It melted." He shakes his head like I've said something crazy.

"That fast?"

"It was barely a dusting, city girl."

A dusting? The snow was several inches thick, but then, there wasn't much snow on the highway when I drove my uncle home from the hospital.

"Come, let's sit." Drake takes the seat closest to the fire. He turns the spit holding the skewers of meat. "Dinner will be done in a few." He fishes around in a bag next to the chair and brings out a bottle of wine. "You said you liked wine. Bert promises this is a good Merlot."

"No whiskey?"

"I figured if you were brave enough to try whiskey, I can try some of this fermented grape juice people rave about." His eyes twinkle with mirth.

This man thinks of everything.

Paper plates, plastic wine glasses, and a roll of paper towels complete our tableware. We sit together, watching the sunset, and feast on steak, grilled onions, tomatoes, and peppers.

The symphony of crickets, birds, cicadas, the soulful lowing of the distant cows, and even the wind whispering in the trees lulls me into a state of deep relaxation.

Drake pours the wine, takes a sip from his cup, then screws his face up with distaste. "This stuff is foul." He tosses the rest of his wine on the ground.

"Hey!" I shout, "Wine foul."

"Yes, the wine is very foul."

"No. I mean you wasted it. This is a fabulous merlot."

"Oh." He looks funny hunching his shoulders and looking apologetic. "You mean, I could've given that to you? If you drink the whole bottle, does that mean you get loose as a goose?"

"You'd like that, wouldn't you?"

"Not really."

"And why's that?"

"Because I'm hoping to get lucky tonight, and that only happens if we're both sober. So, probably good that I dumped that wine."

Holy rocking that confidence, he totally thinks he's getting lucky tonight.

After that kiss in the barn, there's only one way this evening ends, but I can't be too easy.

"But it's an awesome merlot." I push out my lower lip in a pout, then laugh at his expression. He stomps back to the truck and returns with a flask of whiskey.

"And this is awesome whiskey. I'll share if you want some."

"I'm good with the wine." I cup the plastic wine glass, holding it close to my chest.

Whiskey will knock me off my feet. I plan on staying, if not completely sober, then pleasantly flushed with the wine.

We finish our meal, trading conversation with ease. He asks about the moose and my accident, warning me to be careful on the roads. I thank him for helping me and avoid mentioning the wolves.

"How often do you have blizzards like that?"

"Blizzard?" He pokes at a log on the fire. "I don't even think we got a foot of snow."

"If that wasn't a blizzard, what does one look like?"

"I think you're going to be in for a shock once winter comes. We need to put together an emergency kit for you. You'll keep it in your car year-round. Never trust Montana weather. We can have snow in the higher elevations year-round. As the town doc, I assume you'll be making house calls, and you don't want a repeat of that night."

"I suppose so."

Honestly, house calls never crossed my mind. I assumed my practice would be nearly identical to how it was in Redlands. I'd have an office where I saw routine appointments and something for urgent-care after-hour's visits. I figure I'll be tied to a beeper most of the time, taking calls by phone.

But house calls?

That's something I'll have to ask my uncle about. There's so much to learn, and I no longer have the years I thought I'd have to get myself situated. I press a hand to my sternum as a pang of grief rips through me. He's my last living relative, and I'm not ready to lose him.

"What's wrong, city girl?" Drake notices the change in me immediately. He's observant of everything.

"It's nothing." I suck in a breath and make a vague gesture.

"Doesn't look like nothing. You were all sunshine and smiles, then a cloud settled over you. What's wrong?"

"I don't want to bother you ..."

"You're not bothering. Anything that affects you interests me. This may be our first date, but I can already tell where this is headed."

"You can?"

"Sure as shit, I can."

"Very colorful." A smile flips my frown around, and Drake eases back in his seat.

"Now, that's more like it. My girl should never wear a frown. Now, tell me. What's wrong?"

I'm not ready to talk about my uncle. That's something I need to work up to, and I have the perfect way to do that.

"Where is *this* headed?" I gesture between us.

Despite the overland trek, the wolves, and sleeping in the same room—granted in separate twin beds—we're still practically strangers.

"Don't act like you don't feel it." The tone of his voice changes, heating the air while sending shivers down my spine.

He makes me tremble when he touches me and when he speaks to me in that deep baritone. Everything about Drake makes me tremble. He's overwhelming in the best possible way.

"Feel, what?" I'm curious and don't want to guess.

What I know about Drake is he'll answer all my questions directly, never once beating around the bush. I suppose I know him better than I think.

"The air crackles when we're together. Instant chemistry. That kiss in the barn?" He leans back and shakes his head. "Nuclear hot."

"Is that right?"

"Damn straight." He leans toward me and lowers his voice,

making me lean in, narrowing the space between us. That crackling in the air is real. I feel him everywhere. "You may be new in town, but you're mine. I'm staking my claim."

"Yours?"

"Most definitely." He sits back as if he speaks some great truth. No room for disagreement, not with that tone. Not with his unwavering confidence.

"Staking your claim?" I arch a brow, teasing him, but getting more turned on by the minute.

I've never been *claimed* by a man before. I've been possessed. That's what I was to Scott. I was his possession. Somehow, with Drake, being claimed sounds hot.

"Yup. Letting all the single men in town know you're off the market and making sure the married guys know it too. You're stuck with me, Dr. Abby Knight. This is definitely going to be a long-term thing."

"You sound so certain."

"I know what I like, and I know what I need. I'm even willing to forgive your horrible sense of direction." He pokes fun at my direction sense which had me walking away from town after the crash.

"Well, I guess I'll count myself lucky you'll forgive that egregious sin."

"Egregious?" He rolls his eyes and shakes his head. "That's a mighty big word there, city girl. A small-town boy like me might not be able to keep up."

"Somehow, I have a feeling that's not going to be a problem."

"You finished?"

"Um, finished, what?"

"Delaying answering my question? Or have we bantered enough to circle back around to what's bothering you?"

"You, um, you saw that?"

"Luv, you're an open book to me."

"I hope not."

"Why's that?"

"Where's the mystery if you know everything about me?"

"Luv, being an open book only means the pages are available to be read. I'm on page one and loving the way our story is shaping up already. I'm hooked. But don't worry, there's plenty to discover along the way, and I'm in no hurry." He kicks back. "If you're not comfortable sharing, that's okay. You'll tell me when you're ready. In the meantime, we can watch the movie."

"You're nothing like I expect."

"That's good to hear. I've got a few secrets too. You're going to have to read the book to find them."

"I'm looking forward to it."

"Get comfortable. It's a long book."

"How long?"

"A lifetime's worth, I would think."

Whoa!

People talk about feeling butterflies in their stomach; I've got a herd of elephants flying around in mine.

A lifetime?

That should scare me, but honestly?

It feels about right.

"You certainly don't mess around." I shift in my seat, aroused, cautious, and confused.

What is it about this man that hits all my buttons? It's like Drake's got a checklist, crossing off each and every point as he goes down the line. This is far more than country charm.

It's magic.

"Why should I?" He adds a log to the fire and sparks fly up in the air. "I've found the one I want sitting in front of me."

"You don't know anything about me."

"You're fierce. You stared down those wolves."

"I didn't have much of a choice."

"You're adventurous."

"How so?"

"You picked up your big city life to start over in a small town. That takes guts."

"It's a bit more complicated." He doesn't know about Scott.

I ran from Redlands. Scott may think I'll come crawling back to him, but that's never going to happen.

"You're smart. Like not just a little smart, but doctor smart. I respect a woman who takes the world by the horns and isn't afraid to put herself out there. You're not afraid to go after what you want."

"You got all of that from one night?"

"That and more. You're a fighter. Got grit."

"Grit?"

"Yeah, when things get tough, you do what's necessary. Not many chicks would've done what you did without a whole lot of bitching and complaining."

"It's not like that would've helped."

"It wouldn't have, but you figured that out all on your own. You know when you need help, and you're gracious in accepting it. You don't come off as entitled."

"Wow. I've never really thought about any of it like that."

"It doesn't take long to figure out what a person's like, especially when they're under stress. As for me, like I said, once I know what I want, there's no reason not to go for it. And if there's any question about what I want ..." He leans toward me and lowers his voice to a near whisper. "I'm very interested in you, city girl, but if that's too scary for you and you need to pump the brakes, we can do that."

"I appreciate that."

That's what a smart person would do, but I don't disagree with Drake. I can say many of the same things about him. I know his character. I know his strength. I know he's a protector, a hero—if my suspicions about the scar are true. What else do I need to know?

"How about we slow down enough to watch the movie and see how the rest of the night goes."

"Sounds wonderful, and first thing tomorrow, after you know—we're going to town to get you a proper emergency kit for your car."

I don't believe him about the other night not being a blizzard. It sure seemed like a lot of snow. "That sounds like a plan." I don't even blink about the *you know* comment.

We're definitely going to have sex before we leave this place.

"You need to be ready for anything," he says.

With my mind on sex, I can't help the huge grin on my face. Drake reads me like an open book.

"I love where your mind went right there, but I'm talking about your safety. Now, as for your road kit ... Flares would be a good thing. You'll need a blanket, jacket, gloves, gators, and boots. A flashlight too. People need to be able to see you if that ever happens again."

"Well, I wasn't expecting snow in May. I'm just glad I had my suitcases."

"Those layers saved your life."

I empty my wine and lean back with a sigh. "You tell me what to put in this emergency kit, and I'll get it done. I never want to go through that again."

"You never will, city girl. I can guarantee it."

Firelight flickers over his face as I try and parse what he said and what it might mean. There are layers to this man I don't fully grasp, but there's one thing I know for certain.

He's a protector of not only those he cares about, but those he just met. That says more about his character than anything else.

The sun is finally set. Dusk gives way to the darkness of night. The alcohol from the wine relaxes me, and I shed any lingering tension I may have.

He lifts a remote. "Now, what will it be? *Star Wars* marathon or *Star Trek*?"

"Surprise me." I lean back, content and happy for the first time in years.

The opening lines, "*In a galaxy far far away,*" scroll across the screen as Drake lightly strokes the back of my hand.

"I'm glad we met, city girl."

"I'm glad we met too."

17

HEAT

DRAKE AND I WATCH LUKE, LEIA, AND HAN TAKE DOWN THE BATTLE star while I sip wine and he drinks whiskey.

While he loads up the next movie, I pour myself another glass of wine. The bottle's half empty, and I'm at the point where I'm feeling relaxed and comfortable rather than first date jitters.

It's easy with Drake. We fit well together, and it feels as if I've known him far longer than a few days.

Despite the blizzard—and I don't care what Drake says, that was a blizzard—it's pleasantly warm. Not only that, but that cold snap took out the resident mosquito population, allowing me to enjoy the early summer night without being eaten alive.

Drake loads up the next movie, and as Luke meanders around the icy planet of Hoth, Drake reaches for my hand.

Our fingers intertwine as he plays with my hand. He rubs the back of my hand with his thumb, then our pinky fingers interlock, and we simply enjoy the moment and watch the rebels fight against an empire.

My relaxed state deepens. More wine and more whiskey turn our friendly pinky holding into more sensuous glides of fingers and hands. When I glance over at him, Drake's gaze smolders with a banked heat.

Which reminds me how wonderful his mouth feels on my skin when he kisses me.

I loop my index finger around his and lift his hand up between us. Turning our hands palm to palm, I marvel in the differences.

My fingers are long, delicate, and smooth. His are wide, strong, and thickly calloused. Drake's a man who works with his hands. It's evident in everything about him, from his muscular form to the natural confidence which oozes out of every pore.

He's a force of nature and different in every way from other men I've known. The previous men in my life, including Scott, were more concerned about intellectual prowess than anything else.

"Your hand feels good pressed against mine." The smooth cadence of Drake's voice sends a shudder rippling through my body.

He splays his fingers, twining them with mine. Then, he leans over and draws my hand to his mouth, where he gently kisses the inside of my wrist.

My insides do that flippy thing again: butterflies dancing instead of that herd of elephants. A sigh escapes me as Han and Leia fly through a city in the clouds. We're nearly to the end of the *Empire Strikes Back*. I have no idea what time it is, except it must be well past midnight.

After he flutters soft kisses over my inner wrist, I give a little tug, drawing his hand to my mouth, intent on moving this along.

He doesn't fight me. In fact, the eagerness in his expression emboldens me to do something I would otherwise never do. I lift his hand to my mouth and mirror what he did with a soft press of my lips to his inner wrist.

His skin tastes like heaven. He draws back, but I tighten my grip and move my mouth around to his index finger.

Bolder than I've ever been in my life, I slowly take his finger into my mouth, sucking on the tip, licking and flicking the pad of his finger with my tongue.

His eyes widen as I take his entire finger into my mouth, sucking and teasing with a promise I'm excited to deliver on.

Which is very unusual for me.

One of Scott's biggest complaints about our sex life was my lack of desire for less traditional ways to explore and enjoy. But, giving him head never interested me. The few times I did, it was a struggle, and I derived no pleasure from the act. The same went for the reverse. The few times Scott went down on me, it was something to endure rather than enjoy.

"Goddamn, city girl, I hope you're not teasing me." Drake shifts in his seat, making a crude, and very obvious, adjustment to his pants. "You've got me hard and aching."

With my eyes locked to his, I make one more pass up and down his finger, sucking on the tip and giving a little flick with my tongue. I withdraw his finger with a *pop* and sit back with a Cheshire grin on my face.

Then, I very pointedly, cross my arms and face the screen to watch Boba Fett encase Han in carbonite. Tears stream down Leia's face as Chewy howls and wraps his arms around her.

"Oh no, city girl." Drake makes another adjustment and stands. "You're not getting away with that." He takes my hand and yanks me out of my seat.

I tumble into his embrace and right into another toe-curling kiss. As he cups my face and kisses me senseless, I'm reminded of what he said.

Drake has only one speed. There's a little trembling in my body as what that means takes root.

This is it.

Unless, I say no.

But there's no way I'm saying no to this man. My arms wrap around his waist as he steers us clear of the fire and backs me up to the tailgate of his truck. The tailgate is down, and blankets stretch from one wheel well to the other.

Funny, but I don't remember him doing that.

Wedging his hips between my legs, he palms my ass as he pulls our bodies as close as they can possibly get.

"Do you remember what I told you in the barn?" His low, throaty words send a shiver racing through my body.

His exact words? No, I don't remember exactly what he said, but I remember the most important thing.

I grab the hem of my sweater and peel it off my body. My shimmering tank top is next. Shameless, I rip it off my body, revealing the black lace I wore specifically for him.

He stands back, heated gaze taking in the black lace of my bra. Slowly, he hooks his finger under the strap and lifts toward my shoulder.

"Last chance, city girl."

He looks right in my eyes as he draws the strap off my shoulder and down my arm, slowly exposing more of my skin.

"I want this." I want all of it. I'm nervous and excited all at once.

"Music to my ears." He reaches around my back and, with a single flick, releases the hook and latch fastener of my bra.

I tremble as he slowly—so very damn slow—removes the black lace until I'm bare to him from the waist up. He doesn't make a grab for my breasts. Instead, he takes a moment to savor what he sees.

"You're fucking incredible."

Drake leans in and chastely brushes his lips across mine. It's such a soft move that it takes me by surprise, nearly reverent in the execution, but then his lips are on the move, fluttering along my jawline, nibbling on the shell of my ear.

He moves down the arch of my neck, drawing deep moans from me as he sucks on the sensitive skin. His lips press against the hollow of my throat and then move down the center of my chest as I squirm and my nipples tighten with anticipation.

Still no hands. His palms press down on either side of my legs as he kisses me.

His lips travel over the swell of my breast, kissing, suckling, nipping, until his mouth finally, agonizingly, sucks in my nipple.

My breaths quicken as he laves my nipple, teasing the hard nub.

Heat rushes through me, quickening and burning as it settles into a low ache between my legs.

My head tips back as I comb through his hair with my fingers. When he bites down on my nipple, I tug on his hair. The expert application of his tongue is something I've never felt before. I never dreamed such pleasure exists from nipple play alone.

I burn beneath his low, throaty exhales as he moves to my other breast, raining down the same devastation as he did with the first. He deals relentless strokes with that tongue, follows it up with teasing nips of his teeth, all the while torturing me and drowning me in sensation.

His hands move to grip my ass. His fingers dig in as he sucks on my nipple. A sigh escapes me, luxuriating in more sensation than I ever thought possible.

Drake continues, moving according to the pace he sets. His hands move over my hips and down my thighs until they rest at the hem of my skirt.

Slowly, achingly slow, his fingers grip the fabric and draw it up inch by inch. Drake lifts me, drawing my skirt around my ass to expose the black lace thong I wear for him. A low groan of masculine pleasure escapes him.

It's needy, determined, and resolute.

My breasts grow heavy. My nipples ache. A needy pulsation settles between my legs. My fingers catch in his hair as my entire body trembles beneath him. I gulp down a moan as he places his fingers over the small triangle of fabric between my legs.

"Damn, but you're gorgeous, city girl." He lifts away from my breast to capture my lips again.

The moment his mouth covers mine, he yanks the lace to the side and places his fingers over my slit.

I rock against him, needing more stimulation, as his fingers explore my folds and press against the hood of my clit. I curl in my lower lip, biting back a moan as I squirm for him.

"You're wet for me, city girl." His words rush over me as I gulp down another moan. "Should I stop?" He presses his fingers against my slit, teasing.

"Please, don't stop." I've lost count of the number of times he's made me gasp on the cusp of coming undone.

He kisses with a ferocity I've never experienced and explores with determination and intent. Everything he does is calculated to enhance my pleasure. Those wicked fingers of his rub against my folds, taking their damn sweet time as I go crazy with the need for more.

More friction.

More pressure.

Just—more.

"Best words I've ever heard. Luv, I'm not stopping until I'm balls deep, buried in your sweet heat. You're going to feel me for days." With that, he buries his fingers as a quickening rush of exhales spill out of my mouth.

My head tips back. My tits press forward. And that devious tongue of his is on the move again.

Whimpers escape me as he explores with his fingers. I shake as his teeth graze my skin. It doesn't take much before I'm out of breath and panting. Too many pleasurable sensations assault me simultaneously.

He uses his free hand to play with my breast, doubling down on the stimulation of my nipple.

Hard. Peaked. Aroused.

I give a little yelp when he pinches down, holding my poor tortured nipple between his thumb and forefinger. With that pinch of pain, more pleasure courses through me as his other hand, and those talented fingers, work me to a frenzy.

Drake ravishes my pussy, shoving in deep with his fingers, drawing out slow, curling and pressing until he finds *that* spot. A jolt of sensation rocks through me with each determined stroke.

If this is what his fingers feel like, what will it be like when it's his cock instead of his fingers?

Inquiring minds want to know, but not so much as to ask him to stop what he's doing. I've had sex before, but this is unlike anything I've experienced.

My toes curl as his fingers massage and torment. Sensuous heat spreads outward from my core, raw, relentless, and inevitable. A whimper escapes me as pleasure coils and tightens. Getting tighter and tighter as my entire body ignites.

"Drake ... I'm going to ..."

Like a spring releasing its energy all at once, pleasure explodes within me. I cry out and dig my fingernails into a death grip I have on his hair.

My body bucks as his fingers continue their relentless assault until I'm hoarse from my screams and dizzy from the wave of pleasure drowning out all other sensation. My entire body shakes from head to toe as sensual, sexual heat consumes me from the tips of my toes to the top of my head.

I breathe heavily as the determined motion of his fingers subsides. My entire body, muscles and bones, liquefy in a languid state of being. It's the first time in my life where sex leaves me a moaning puddle of quivering flesh.

Drake slowly withdraws his fingers while I curl against him, chest heaving, body quaking, blissfully satisfied for the first time ever in my life.

Who knew an orgasm could feel that good? Those paltry things I've felt before hold nothing to the deft skill of the man who played my body like a virtuoso.

"You going to be all right?" Drake runs his fingers through my hair, gathering it to hang down my back. His lips feather across my shoulder in reverent worship.

"That was ..." I huff and puff, still catching my breath.

We're close. He smells amazing, bold and powerful, dark and seductive. I wrap my arms around his neck and curl into him.

Drake looks at me with smoldering lust filling his gaze. I take him in, memorizing every detail from the slanted scar marring the perfection of his face, to the rigid muscles twining up his neck. His entire body vibrates with need.

"Yes, luv?"

"Incredible," I say the word with a sigh of contentment. "Simply incredible."

"If you thought that was incredible, wait until I slide inside you. I'm looking forward to this, city girl."

"Did you bring ..."

"Protection?" His brow arches with amusement. "You bet, but we're not ready for that just yet."

Not ready?

18

CHEMISTRY

DRAKE NUZZLES MY NECK AND GENTLY CUPS MY BREAST. "YOU'RE gorgeous when you come." The roughness of his thumb grazes against my tender nipple, sending a jolt of electricity to my core. "So fucking sexy."

I look away, shy and a bit awkward. Talking about sex isn't really my thing. His thumb rubs against my nipple, slowly rolling it back and forth. When I reach for the fly of his pants, Drake draws back.

"Oh, luv, we'll get to that." With an authoritative hand, he pushes me back.

Not sure what he's doing, I resist. This is the point when he's supposed to strip, put on a condom, and fuck me.

Drake increases the pressure on my chest as my brows pinch together with confusion.

"Stop," he says, more authoritative, more demanding.

Totally sexy.

I love a man who knows what he wants. It's a major turn on. The ones who bumble about—my ex comes to mind—ruin the mood.

Drake amplifies my desire, arousing me more with his voice and his commands than the way his finger plays with my poor, tortured nipple.

"Stop, what?"

The palm of his hand presses with greater force against my sternum.

"Stop fighting me."

"I'm not ..."

He presses harder, and my brows knit together even more confused.

"You're resisting me, luv." His head cants to the side. "Relax. I promise I'll make this good for you."

Better than that orgasm? It's not possible.

"But I thought ..."

"Don't think, city girl. All you need to do is feel. Let me take the lead." He pushes a little harder while my muddled mind tries to parse what he means.

Why does he want me to lean back when it makes more sense to scoot my ass forward on the tailgate, wrap my legs around his waist, and have sex like that? The heights look like they match.

My brain does a deep dive into angles and heights. Drake taps me on the forehead.

"Disengage that beautiful brain from your body, city girl. Surrender. Trust that I know what I'm doing."

I've never been this passive during sex in my life. It's not what I'm used to. I'm used to getting down to business. The quicker I got the guy off, the sooner I could get back to what I was doing. It's no surprise my sex life is lackluster at best.

But, I trust Drake. I trust him more than any other man I've known, which is shocking considering we—you know—just met.

Slowly, I surrender to his will, leaning back until my back hits the soft padding of the covers he laid out in the bed of his truck. Bending at the knees, my feet dangle off the back of the tailgate.

Since I'm a little out of my element, I kick out my left foot and then my right, letting my legs swing. Drake places his hand over my shins, stilling the nervous movement.

"There you go." Drake leans over me, a satisfied smirk on his face. "Relax and let go, luv. All I want you to do is feel."

"But what about you?"

"We're getting to that. No reason to rush to the finish line. This isn't a race."

I want to ask what I should do but decide I'm wrong about him fucking me on the tailgate. The truck is taller than I thought.

Maybe he's worried about the angles, and the relative heights of our respective parts? I place my hands on the covers with the thought of pushing up and back, thinking to move farther into the bed of the truck so he can join me.

The moment I do, Drake grabs my knees and yanks me toward him. It confuses me because that's not what I was expecting, but then Drake blows my mind yet again.

He puts his hands on my inner thighs, spreads my legs, then hooks my knees over his shoulders.

Before I can process what he's about to do, Drake buries his face between my legs.

My body bucks, which only lifts my pussy up to his face. The scruff of his beard rubs against my inner thighs, burning and scraping, but the moment his tongue licks along my seam, I forget all about that and focus on the heat of his mouth as he ravishes me once more.

I'm not a fan of oral sex. Or rather, I wasn't until now.

This is unlike anything I've experienced.

With his hands on my thighs, my entire body quivers with delicious sensation. My knees drape over his shoulders, fully supported, as his tongue works even more devastating magic.

I surrender to the moment, doing what he says, and turn into a carnal thing. My body bucks and thrashes. My back bows and my hips move in a sinuous dance. I reach for his head, digging my fingers into his thick, midnight-black hair, and hold on for the best ride of my life.

He leaves nothing unexplored, mercilessly fucking my pussy with his tongue and laving my clit with tantalizing strokes. Like a man starved for food, he eats my pussy, groaning against me, until our bodies find a rhythm.

My pelvis grinds against his face. My heels dig into his back. My toes curl until barely human, guttural sounds emanate from my throat. He turns me into a wanton creature, focused solely on the pleasure of my flesh.

An incredible rush of heat builds within me, tightening until I'm breathless and panting with the need to come. I'm unable to pull the air I need into my lungs for the scream that waits on the precipice of what I know will be an incredible release.

Something inside of me snaps and lets go. Pleasure sweeps through me for the second time.

Only this orgasm is more intense than the first. His deft touch, with that devilish tongue, licks me through and past the firestorm sweeping through me.

As the quaking in my body stills, Drake looks up, my wetness on his lips, with the most satisfied smirk I've ever seen plastered on his face.

"Drake, that was beyond amazing, but if you don't fuck me right now, I'm going to kill you."

The aftershocks of that orgasm race through me, and I want to feel him inside of me before this feeling subsides.

"Sit up, city girl, and slide to the edge." He disentangles our bodies and takes a step back. While I move, he rips open a foil pack and unzips.

My eager eyes wait for the first time I get to see him. It takes a breath, or two, for his full length to free itself from the confines of his zipper.

He's hard, growing harder as I watch. Plump head, thick, ropey veins, his shaft stands primed and ready. He sheaths himself, sliding the condom on like a pro, while my hand flies to my throat when the full impact hits me.

"How's that going to fit?"

Drake glances at me, eyes hooded with lust, swirling with desire, as a low chuckle escapes him.

"Don't worry. It'll fit, we just gotta go slow."

As a doctor, I've seen plenty of flaccid and semi-flaccid penises. It comes with the job, seeing how half my patients are male. Drake certainly puts most men to shame.

As I watch, in shock, horror, and with guilty pleasure—I wonder if I hit the jackpot. How is that going to fit not only in my pussy, but in my mouth?

For the first time, in a very long time, the thought of giving head excites me. To be able to control such a monster—to deliver that kind of pleasure—the thought of it sets off that needy pulse between my legs again.

Drake fists his shaft, stroking it lazily as I watch. "I take it you like what you see?"

"I've never ..." I reach forward, needing to feel the steely hardness of his cock.

Drake removes his hand and waits patiently for me to touch him. Moments before my fingers connect with his hard length, I draw back as if stung. His low chuckle brings my gaze up to his face.

"It's not going to bite you." His hand shoots out and wraps around my wrist. With our gazes interlocked, he brings my hand to his cock. "Just like I don't do slow, I don't do tentative either. If you're going to hold my cock, grip it like you mean it. Hold it tight." He shows me what he means.

When my grip weakens, his hand is there, wrapping around mine, demonstrating how hard I can grip him. His eyes slide shut and his head tips back.

"Just like that." Then he glides my hand along his shaft, tighter than I would've thought comfortable, until we're at the tip. "Don't be afraid to roll your palm against the tip. And don't worry about your nails." He curves my fingers, digging my nails against the underside of his cock. "Pain is but another flavor of pleasure. Dig in, scrape if you want. I'll let you know if you're being too rough."

He shows me exactly what he means.

"And what about my teeth?" He opens one eye, that grin of his going wide. "Oh, I like it rough. The rougher the better. The only question is this."

"What?"

"What about you? Are you a slow and easy kind of girl? Or are you willing to get a bit freaky with some creative and vigorous sex?"

My standard go-to answer would be slow and easy, but I've learned my thoughts about sex may not necessarily be the end-all be-all of what it can be.

"You said to trust you." I cup his face with my free hand.

"You sure about that?"

"Never been more sure." I bite my lower lip and hesitate. "But what if it's too much?"

"Luv, if it gets too intense, tap my shoulder twice. I'll slow down. If you need things to stop, just say the word."

"Okay."

The entire time we talk, he guides my hand up and down his cock. His hips engage, thrusting forward and drawing back.

"What if you're too big?"

"I won't be." His voice grows hoarse as the stimulation to his cock continues.

He releases my hand and braces against the tailgate, closing in on me and crowding me with his broad frame.

Without his help, I can't squeeze as tight as him, but I try out what he said and drag my nail down the undermost side of his shaft where it's most sensitive.

Drake buries his chin into my neck, convulsing with pleasure.

"Fuuuck, but that feels good." He nuzzles my neck while I continue stroking him.

The more I have my hand on him, the bolder I get. I want to suck him, but I'm not really sure how that will work given our current positions. My legs spread wide as he stands between them. My feet dangle like before. There's no rush, and it feels as if we have all the time in the world.

A hypnotic trance slips over me as my hand glides up and then down his shaft. My breathing relaxes. My lids bounce as my eyes close. I tip my head back as a sigh escapes me.

Drake's arms shoot out. He grasps my hips and lifts me up and into the air. I cry out in surprise as my hands grab at his neck. He takes several steps back, holding me in his arms.

His erection bobs between us, brushing against my ass. Without a word, his biceps flex. I rise. Then he holds incredibly still as the tip of his dick slips into position. Just the tip pokes against my wet folds.

"Remember," he struggles to speak. "Two taps if it's too much."

Two taps? I've already forgotten why I would do that, but then the most intense burn makes me cry out.

He lowers me down, using gravity to accomplish the inevitable. It's been some time since I've had sex—and never like this—and I can't help but think back to the last time.

It wasn't good.

Drake's massive cock slides into me, stretching the tight walls of my pussy as he relentlessly forces his way inside.

"Doing okay, luv?"

I give a tight nod and bite my tongue. Holy hell, it hurts, but it's going to be magical if I can get through this little bit. If a ten-pound baby can pass through a woman's vagina, I'm sure I can manage Drake's well-endowed cock.

Totally *not* what I should be thinking about while having sex, but my mind goes off on random tangents, and ... Holy hell!

A ripple of pleasure rushes through me, making me gasp.

"What's wrong?" Drake tightens his hold on me.

"Nothing—it feels amazing."

And that's the truth.

What was that? A micro-orgasm? Is that even a thing?

Drake kisses me, then slowly relaxes his biceps. As he does, gravity does its thing. I slowly, inextricably, slide down the steel shaft of his cock until he's fully buried inside of me.

A jolt of pleasure shoots through my body. I'm not doing a thing, yet I'm strung out and panting with the deliciousness of all the sensations rioting through my body.

I feel him *everywhere.*

"Shit, city girl, you feel fucking amazing. So hot. So warm. So fucking tight. Still doing okay?"

I love the way he checks in on me. He's worried, wanting to make this good for me. Which makes me wonder if he's not self-conscious about his size.

It's a lot to take in.

A smile curls all the way up to my eyes. I've never had a man with a big dick before and it lives up to the hype. Add in Drake's rugged good looks, his sensitivity melded with his feral masculinity, and I'm basically in Nirvana.

"I'm good."

Drake begins to move. He stands solidly. Lifting and lowering me up and down his cock, pleasure builds and builds until a third orgasm spirals me into oblivion.

He pumps me up and down as sensation riots through. Every cell in my body sizzles as he thrusts harder, rocking our bodies together.

Picking up speed, his breathing turns erratic as my entire body liquefies in his hands, completely and absolutely overcome with sensation.

His breaths turn to deep grunts as he fucks me, thrusting savagely. He jerks out, lifting just high enough to slam me back down on his cock. That burn is nothing but a memory as pleasure coils and tightens.

Tears swim in my eyes as his raw, sexual need flames across my skin. Deeper and harder, his hips piston furiously as he chases his release. My entire body is aflame, consumed by pleasure, as Drake finally releases inside of me.

From head to toe, I'm spent.

He very carefully walks us back to the tailgate, where he sets me down. His cock softens and slips out. While he takes care of the condom, I scoot all the way back into the bed of the truck, smoothing out the blankets and fluffing the pillows.

He turns off the generator and tidies up our camp. I guess we're done with movie night. The truck rocks as he vaults into the back. On hands and knees, he prowls toward me. His entire body covers mine. For a moment, he stares at me, then his head lowers.

Drake captures my mouth, kissing me with tenderness and maybe something more.

I've been blissfully fucked by a wonderful man. Talk about mind-blowing. Nothing can bring me down from this high.

Absolutely nothing.

He rolls to his side and grips my hand as we stare up at the night sky, saying nothing as we simply connect.

Soon, his breathing slows. His hard body relaxes, and his grip on my hand eases, then finally releases as the slumber takes him under.

Careful not to wake him, I draw up a blanket to cover us both. Then I stare at the heavens, comforted with the knowledge that I made the right decision moving to Peace Springs.

I watch him sleep for a while. His chest rises and falls in a slow, easy rhythm. At some point, I drift off.

The first rays of dawn spread across the sky, light greens, yellows, and the faintest pink wake me from the best sleep I've had in years.

Drake's arm drapes heavily across my midsection. His leg curls around mine, caging me in, and makes me feel wonderfully safe.

I could lift his arm and disentangle myself from his leg, but I'm not ready for this to end. He wakes and pulls me close, makes love to me as the dawn breaks. Time stands still as we lose ourselves in each other. Eventually, we head back to civilization.

We pack and load everything into the back of the pickup. Then we drive back to town in companionable silence, where we stop at Shelly's Diner for her magic pancakes.

19

HOME

Drake pulls up to my uncle's house and walks me to the front door. He leans in close. I think he's going to kiss me, but he dodges to the side to whisper in my ear.

"I had the best night." He teasingly nips at my ear. "Can't wait for our next movie night."

"When is that?" My reply is energetic.

Enthusiastic.

His low, throaty chuckle brings a smile to my face. "Damn, but you're adorable." He taps the tip of my nose. "I've got work on the ranch that needs doing, then I promised Bert to help mend some of the fences on his property. That's going to keep me busy until sundown." He peers up at the sky, covering his eyes as he tracks the sun. "You kept me up late, city girl. I'm falling behind in my chores."

"Chores?" I lift on tiptoe, cupping his chin as I place a chaste kiss on his mouth. "You're a grown man. You don't do chores."

"Chores. Work. It's all the same. I'd love to see you tonight, but I'll probably be working late."

I bite my lower lip, unable to stop the show of my disappointment, but then he laughs again. Drake reaches for me and pulls me tight to his chest.

"You're my permanent Friday and Saturday night date. How does Friday sound?"

"It sounds like a really long time from now."

His lips curve. The scaring on his face distorts the smile, but his eyes twinkle with mirth. Someday, I'll be bold enough to ask about that scar.

"If I can, I'll call sooner. But for now, let's plan on Friday."

I pick at his shirt, remembering what his skin felt like beneath my palms. "Another movie night?"

"Yeah, we'll have another movie night. Minus the movie part." The wicked grin on his face turns my insides to mush.

Apparently, Drake turns me into a needy, sex-crazed lunatic. Which is totally fine by me.

"Sounds wonderful." Thinking about sex with Drake sets off needy pulsations between my legs. I could go another few rounds with him.

Drake leans down, kisses me senseless, then waits for me to open the door. After I head in, I glance back outside and watch his truck disappear around the corner. With a deep sigh, I shut the door and lean my forehead against the warm wood.

What an incredible night.

A throat clears behind me, and I spin around. My uncle sits on the couch, looking gaunt and pale. A threadbare afghan covers his lap, one I recognize from when I was a kid. My aunt knitted that for him, giving it to him as a gift.

While my heart breaks with his illness, he appears at peace. That makes some of this easier for me. I'm not ready to lose my uncle, but his entire being lit up when he said he would soon join my aunt. I have to find comfort in his joy.

"Late night?" He takes a sip of water and waits for my answer.

"You didn't wait up for me, did you?"

"No. I just got up. Made some breakfast. It's in the kitchen but might be cold by now."

"I had breakfast at Shelly's Diner."

"Ah ..." He takes another sip while I wait for him to ask the obvious, but my uncle's having too much fun watching me squirm.

Why do I feel like a recalcitrant teenager who got caught sneaking home? The silence is killing me.

My uncle takes another slow sip, eyes simmering with amusement as I pick at nonexistent lint on my skirt.

"What?" I can't stand it any longer and wring my fingers together.

"Nothing." Another sip. "You're a grown woman."

"Aren't you going to ask where I've been?"

"Not my place."

Not his place? He's sure looking at me like my father used to when I broke curfew growing up.

"So, you're not going to ask?"

Another sip. He smooths out the afghan on his lap, pointedly not looking at me. He picks up the book he was reading, turns the page, then looks back up at me.

"Do you want me to ask?" He turns his attention back to the book, pointedly ignoring me.

Do I?

It's a fair question, with an obvious answer. Uncle Pete and I don't have much time left together, months if we're lucky. Pancreatic cancer is a relentless monster. I want to share this with him. Not the sex part, but meeting Drake. Going out on a date. Having fun.

Not worrying about when the next punch will come.

I cross the room and plop down into the chair opposite him. "I was out with Drake."

"Drake?"

"You know, the one who helped me the other night?" I told my uncle all about the mysterious man who shot the wolves and saved me from the blizzard.

"I do. I know him well, as a matter of fact." He turns his attention back to the book, looking disinterested. Only my uncle is a horrible liar. He's keenly interested in what I have to say.

"And?"

"And, what?" I worry my lower lip between my teeth, anxiously waiting for my uncle to ask me something—anything—about Drake.

He's having fun messing with me.

"What do you think about him?" I bounce on the balls of my feet, urging him to pump me for information.

"Are you asking for my opinion or my blessing?"

"I dunno." I shrug and think about his question. What do I want? "Is he a nice guy?"

"Was he nice to you?"

"Yes."

More than nice.

Although, when I really think about it, nice guys usually don't fuck on the first date. For that matter, nice girls don't either.

"Then I think very well of him." My uncle is purposefully hedging. "He's one of the good ones."

Finally.

It's nice to hear Uncle Pete commit to an answer. If he thinks Drake is one of the good ones, then I have nothing to worry about. There's only one problem.

Drake's not a *nice* guy.

Although, he's not pinging any warning bells in my head. Not that failing to set off alarms means anything.

Scott didn't either.

I'm a horrible judge of character.

Scott's abuse came on gradually, so much so that I didn't recognize it for what it was. Even after the second visit to the emergency room, I still made excuses, blaming myself for what happened.

"Uncle Pete, I need to tell you something."

"What's up?" He puts the book down and gives me his full attention.

"I want to tell you about Scott."

His brows tug together, and the gentle smile on his face disappears. I've told no one about the abuse.

It's my ugly secret, and I don't fully understand all the emotions behind it. While I know, intellectually, that none of it is my fault, I bear a tremendous amount of guilt.

Why didn't I leave sooner?

What did I do to deserve it?

Why did I keep excusing what he did?

Why did I keep forgiving him?

Why did I, a smart, professional woman, not realize how toxic my relationship was?

In many ways, I feel like a failure, ashamed of that piece of my past. But after all the berating, I focus on the positives.

The biggest positive sits across from me. As I tell my uncle about the abuse, my hands tremble, and my body shakes.

"Your invitation couldn't have come at a better time." I sit back and take in a deep, cleansing breath.

That felt good. Like really good. Telling my uncle about what happened lifts a terrible weight off my shoulders. I feel lighter, less burdened. It finally feels as if I can move on.

"Oh, Abby, I'm so sorry. I had no idea." He makes a move to stand.

I think he wants to come to me, give me a hug, but he's too weak. The cancer gets worse day by day.

I hang my head and stare at my hands. I trace the lines on my palm, remembering the way Drake kissed every inch.

"Please tell me Drake is one of the good ones." I can't bear another broken relationship.

And Uncle Pete should know about Drake. As the town doc, he knows everyone in town, and if what he said earlier is true, he knows where the bodies are buried. Metaphorically, that is.

"You have nothing to worry about with Drake."

"What can you tell me about him?"

"How much do you know?"

"Very little."

I let a man, who I don't know, fuck me into oblivion. For someone who made a vow to steer clear of romantic entanglements, I certainly stepped right into one hell of a mess.

Relationships founded on physical attraction alone seldom stand the test of time.

That's my mother speaking. Her words of wisdom fill my head and break my heart. I miss her terribly.

It feels as if I've made my first colossal mistake. Unlike Scott, this won't be one I can run away from. Peace Springs is my future. I'm stuck here.

"Drake is a good man. Gentle. Kind to animals. Good with people. He goes out of his way to protect others. Joined the military, did a lot of stuff he can't talk about. He's harder now, smiles less, but his heart is in the right place."

"Is that where he got the scar? The military?"

"That came later."

"What happened?"

"That feels like something you should ask him, but as far as whether he's one of the good guys, you can't do better than that man. He's seen a lot, been through a lot, lost more than anyone should. He's an incredibly hard worker. Manages one of the largest ranches in the local area and still helps out where he can."

"Like Bert's llama farm?"

My uncle laughs. "Technically, it's a llama ranch, but yeah. Ever since Bert's wife and son died, Drake's been helping him out."

Wife and son? "That sounds tragic."

"Sorry, I've probably said too much. Curse of being the town doc. People tell me all kinds of things. Speaking of, I thought we might head into the office. I've got some things I need to take care of."

I look at him and wonder if that might not be the best thing. His strength is failing. But that's not my decision to make.

"I need to take a shower." I hold back a smile as to why that might be. "Give me a little bit?"

"No rush, sweetie."

I head to my room and take a shower. When I remove my clothes, I breathe in the lingering scent of Drake on the fabric. Part of me doesn't want to wash him off my skin, but it's time to get to work.

The faster I learn the ropes of my uncle's practice, the easier things will be in the long run.

20

WORK

LESS THAN AN HOUR LATER, I'M SHOWERED, DRESSED, AND EVEN PUT ON a bit of makeup. When I head into the living room, my uncle isn't there, but there are sounds coming from the kitchen. I head in there, where he's cleaning up his breakfast dishes.

"Can I help?"

"No, that's the last little bit. You ready to head in to work?"

I'm nervous and excited at the same time. He says work, which makes me think this isn't a casual visit.

"How many patients do you have scheduled?"

"Just a few. I've blocked off my mornings for the foreseeable future. Mornings are the worst for me."

I can understand that.

"I'd love to help out. No better way than to jump in and get my feet wet."

"That would be very helpful. And I agree. We still have some time before the first appointment. I thought I'd show you some of the not-so-fun aspects of the practice."

It's another reminder I'm in over my head. In Redlands, all I did was show up and see patients. I didn't have to worry about running a business. I was an employee.

Not a business owner.

"That's what I'm most worried about."

"What's that, hun?"

"The business side of things. Do you think I should take some classes?"

"You don't need to do that. I've got a business manager. Sara takes care of most things. She handles the books, does most of the coding, and deals with all the insurance claims. The office practically runs itself, but there are a few things I need to show you. And of course, we'll want to introduce you to the specialists you'll be referring patients to."

"Okay."

"Everyone knows you're coming. I've been talking you up ever since you agreed, but we'll want to make introductions before ..." His voice trails off, and just like him, I don't want to hear the end of that particular sentence.

With that heaviness weighing me down, I force a smile to my face. "I'm eager to get started."

Which is the truth.

It's been well over a week since I fled Redlands. I took my time driving up the coast, needing those few days to figure out what the hell I was going to do.

My job is the best on the planet. Helping others to stay healthy makes me feel good. Helping those who are sick manage chronic conditions, or recover from an illness, is the greatest gift I've been given. I consider myself blessed.

That's all to say, I'm excited to get back to work.

There's one major problem.

When Uncle Pete and I go outside, all four tires of the Jeep are flat.

"That's odd." Uncle Pete walks around the car, looking at the tires. He gives them a kick, slowly—agonizingly slow—he bends down to inspect the rear left tire. "I don't see any punctures."

I crouch next to him and examine the tire. Unless it's a massive rip in the rubber, I have no idea what to look for. Uncle Pete does. He checks the inflation valves on all the tires. He stands and glances up and down the street.

"It was probably some kids playing a prank," he says.

"Why do you say that?"

He points to the tires like I know what he means.

"Someone let out the air."

"Why would they do that?"

"Just kids pranking and having fun. We can take my car. I'll text Henry Watkins and see if he can't come by with his compressor and fix that for you."

"That sounds great."

Not wanting to waste any more time, we take his car. Seeing how unsteady he is on his feet, I offer to drive.

It's a little past eleven by the time we make it to his office. This time, the people aren't strangers. I recognize faces from earlier but lost all their names. Fortunately, Uncle Pete reintroduces me.

The office receptionist, Angie, greets me with bright eyes and a warm smile.

"So nice to see you again, Dr. Knight."

"Oh please, call me Abby."

Angie's gaze shifts to my uncle and her brows wing up. He coughs beside me.

"While we like to keep things informal between the staff, at work, we're more professional. It's important for the patients to know you as Dr. Knight, rather than Abby. If the staff calls you by your first name, the patients will internalize that. It's going to be really important to establish your reputation."

"That's Dr. Bateman's way of saying not only are you pretty, but you're young. A lot of our patients are older, and you know how that goes."

"I suppose so. It didn't really occur to me."

"When we head out for a girl's day on the town, first names work fine, but it's easier for me to stick with Dr. Knight here. Don't want to slip."

"And that goes for the rest of the staff." Uncle Pete emphasizes the point, making sure I understand.

"Gotcha."

Uncle Pete guides me to his office in the back of the clinic. It's a corner office with huge windows looking out onto a grassy lawn. Towering oak trees provide shade to clusters of benches that sit beneath them.

Next to his office is Sara's office. Only slightly smaller than his, potted plants crowd the window ledge. More plants take over the tops of her filing cabinets and spill over the side tables, bracketing a well-worn, leather sofa.

Uncle Pete knocks on her door. A few years younger than my uncle, Sara's long, salt and pepper hair hangs freely over her shoulders and down her back in springy curls. She looks up and pushes on the bridge of her glasses.

"Pete!" She stands and moves around her desk. "You made it." Arms outstretched, she folds him into a gentle hug.

I get the gentle part. Uncle Pete's losing weight at an alarming rate. He kisses her cheek then turns to me.

"Meet my niece, Abby Knight."

Sara takes my hand in hers. Rather than shaking, she clasps both hands around mine and holds me with one of the brightest smiles I've ever seen.

"I've heard so much about you. Pete goes on and on. He's very proud of you, and I know you're going to fit in just fine."

It's one of the warmest welcomes I've ever received.

Things are different here.

The people are different.

Warmer.

Happier.

They roll out the welcome mat, not because they have to, but because it's what they do.

Peace Springs is different.

It's home.

"Sara, I thought maybe you could sit with Abby and show her what you do. I need to catch up on my charting. Maybe we can head to Eddie's for lunch?"

"That sounds wonderful." Sara drags a chair around to her desk and pats the seat. "Come here, let me show you everything you need to know."

"I think that's going to take a very long time."

Sara's eyes shimmer as my uncle excuses himself. The moment we're alone, she looks at me. "That man is a saint, but he needs to stop coming to work."

"I'm not sure I can stop him, but maybe the best way to do that is to get me up and running as soon as possible. He said he has patients this afternoon. I was hoping he'd let me see some of them."

"Oh, that's great. Let me suggest it after lunch. You know how men are. Pete is a trooper, but he doesn't know how to let go." She settles down in her plush office chair and pats the seat beside her. "Let's start with our EMR."

For the next hour, Sara shows me everything I need to know about the electronic medical record system Uncle Pete and the rest of the staff use to chart their patient encounters.

Proficient in that aspect of the job, it doesn't take long before I feel comfortable with the EMR they use.

"Best part of it is that it's the same software they use in St. Vincent's in Billings. Which means all the consults, referrals, and inpatient medical stays are available to you."

Sara shows me how to access those records as well. One of the benefits of EMRs is they can be shared with other physicians and medical practices.

"There's a lot more to show you." Sara glances at her watch. "But if we're going to make it back before your first patient, we should get a move on."

"I'll grab my uncle." I replace the chair back against the wall, then head next door.

"Uncle Pete? Are you ready for lunch?"

He sits behind his massive desk and looks up from the computer screen. The blue glow from the monitor makes his skin look even more pale than usual.

"Ah yes." He glances at his screen and exits out of the EMR.

He wobbles a bit when he stands. I hold back rushing to help him, weighing the pros and cons of treating him like an invalid.

Sara joins us, glancing over my shoulder as my uncle slowly crosses the room.

"Sara, did you happen to ask Pamela and Craig to join us?"

"I did not, but let me see if they're finished with their last patients."

While Sara goes to check, I bend my elbow and silently offer it to him for support. Without a word, my uncle takes the assist.

"Pamela and Craig? I don't remember them." My previous visit was short, and I'm horrible with names.

"Pamela Seagars and Craig Moran are your family medicine nurse practitioners. You're really going to enjoy working with them." He leans on me more than I expect, but that's okay.

We meet up with Sara and two others in the front office. Sara makes the introductions while I keep my uncle steady on his feet. A man with sandy blond hair, freckles, and baby blue eyes, extends his hand in greeting.

"Welcome to Peace Springs. I've been looking forward to meeting you. If you need anything, don't hesitate to call." Craig isn't much older than me. His grip is firm and welcoming.

I'm going to enjoy working with him.

Pamela greets me next. With short brown hair cut into a bob, her smile comes easily. It settles in the gentle laugh lines crinkling her eyes.

"How about Abby and Pete ride with me," Sara says, "and the rest of you go together?"

We split up into our respective cars and head off to Eddie's Soda Shoppe. It's just like I remember it with its red and white checkerboard floor. Metal stools set around the counter with bright red seats.

We find a set of tables, rearranging them to accommodate our group. And just like many summers long ago, I order a vanilla milkshake to dip my fries in.

Everyone but Uncle Pete gives me a strange look. He smiles, grabs a fry, and dips it in the chilly milkshake. It's the best way to eat French fries, something he taught me when I turned five.

Lunch is great.

In addition to my fries, I gulp down a juicy cheeseburger and listen to all the advice they give about moving to Peace Springs. It's a close-knit group, and while we talk about everything and anything, there's one topic that doesn't come up. No one speaks about what happens after my uncle is gone.

But then, they've had longer to deal with that news and process it.

We finish up lunch and, as we head outside, a large man blocks the doorway. My heart leaps to my throat when I realize it's Drake. He turns sideways, letting the others pass.

Towering over Craig, Drake tips his hat as he says hello. Craig clasps Drake's hand and they exchange a few words. They're obviously friends.

Pamela laughs at something Drake whispers in her ear. Angie is all atwitter, laughing and blushing as she, unashamedly, grips his bicep. Sara slaps Drake on the chest, laughing at whatever it is he says. Which leaves me and Uncle Pete as the last to exit Eddie's Soda Shoppe.

The moment Drake's gaze turns to me, my stomach flutters, and my pulse kicks into high gear. My entire body trembles with the crazy power this man holds over me. Drake closes the distance, eyes soft with a smile on his face.

"It's nice to see you up and about, Dr. Bateman."

"It's good to be seen."

My uncle extends a hand, which Drake takes with great care. He doesn't shake it the way he did with Craig. Drake is gentle, reverent, and exceedingly careful not to hurt my uncle.

"It's nice to see you again, Abby."

Words fail me. My cheeks feel nuclear hot, which means I must be blushing ten ways to Sunday.

"I hear you saved my girl." Uncle Pete speaks when it's obvious I've forgotten how to form words.

"I agree with only half of that statement."

"How so?" My uncle's reply comes out a challenge, but then his eyes widen. He wings up an inquisitive brow, looking between me and Drake. A smile brightens his eyes.

"All I did was get rid of some vermin. As for your niece, she's *my girl*." Drake moves around my uncle to tug me tight to his side. It's a chaste hug but laced with the ferocity of Drake's desire.

Not only have I lost the ability to speak, but swallowing appears to be beyond my abilities at the moment. My mouth feels incredibly dry as I work to swallow the lump in my throat and calm down some of the nervous energy swirling in my body.

"It's a relief to know she's in good hands." My uncle's comment takes me by surprise.

It does feel as if I'm being handed off.

The *men* talk about me as if I'm not there. Normally, that would piss me off, but I have a sense there's more going on in the words they say.

"I should thank you for bringing her to me."

"I suppose life just kind of works out like that." My uncle releases the death grip he has on my arm and shambles out of the restaurant. Sara rushes over to him, proffering his arm to steady his gait.

I look between my uncle and Drake, then crane my neck until I capture Drake's smoldering gaze.

"What was all of that?"

"Nothing." His smoldering gaze does indecent things to my insides.

I'm lava hot. Molten desire swims in my veins. Drake is simply that overwhelming, but what was all that subtext between him and my uncle?

"Like hell that was nothing." I prop my fists on my hips.

"What?" He blinks like an innocent baby, only Drake's no innocent.

"The whole *my girl* and *she's in good hands?*" On an impish impulse, I reach out and pinch his nipple.

I've never seen a man lift on tiptoe like that. Drake practically levitates.

His large hand clamps down on mine. Pressure applied to my wrist makes my fingers let go.

"Fair's fair." I grin up at him, pleased with myself.

"Don't think I won't make you pay for that. As for your uncle, don't worry about him. I may, or may not, have asked for his permission to take you out."

"You did, what?"

"You heard me."

When did he do that? Because a second ago, Uncle Pete said he *heard* Drake saved me. Which makes it seem like this is the first time they've talked about me, but Drake says otherwise. I'm very confused.

"What I heard is that you asked his permission."

"You're in Peace Springs, city girl. We do things a bit differently around here. I wanted your uncle's blessing before I moved forward, and he gave it."

"He did?"

"That and more."

"Do I even want to ask what that means?" My attention shifts outside to my uncle while I figure out what the two of them are up to.

Sara and Uncle Pete stoop over, looking at her car. Sara drags her finger across the front passenger side door all the way to the back of the car.

"Probably not." Drake's grin is positively sinful. If his smirk wasn't so damn sexy, I'd smack it off his face. As it is, I melt for him.

So damn cheesy, but true.

I melt for him.

"What the hell does that mean?" I know I shouldn't ask, but I can't help but dig that hole.

"Only that Doc Bateman is a very intuitive man."

"That *literally* means nothing."

Drake's insufferable.

Completely insufferable.

"Remember that book I was talking about?"

"You mean the one about me being an open book to you?"

"More like us being an open book to each other. That's buried deep in chapter twelve. You're going to have to stick around to turn all those pages." He points toward my uncle who slowly lowers into Sara's car. "Give me a sec."

Drake kisses my brow, then jogs out to Sara's car. They put their heads together and glance up and down the street. Drake bends over, also looking at the paint.

I join them.

"Hey, what's up?" My cheery voice doesn't match the frown on Sara's face.

"Some punk kid keyed my car." She points to a long scratch in the paint. "I'm so pissed."

In broad daylight?

Drake's brows push together as he scans the street. I thought small towns were supposed to be safe, but it looks like that may no longer be true.

"How often does something like this happen around here?"

I liked living in Redlands. It's a great location, a couple of hours from the beach as well as the mountains, but I never really felt safe when I was alone.

At night, I thought long and hard about going anywhere alone. The parking lots needed to be well lit, and there had to be a lot of people around. To see vandalism like this in Peace Springs is worrisome.

"Don't worry, Sara." Drake stands. "I'll call Henry and we'll get it fixed."

"Thank you." When Sara rests her hand on Drake's arm, the urge to knock her hand off his arm overwhelms me. Which is weird. I'm not the jealous type, but Drake's mine.

Sara moves around to the driver's side, leaving Drake and me staring at each other.

"I really wish I'd known you were coming here. I would've joined you." Drake takes my hand in his, threading his fingers with mine.

"That would've been nice, but it was a spontaneous thing."

"I had some errands to run in town, but I need to head back out." Drake grips the back of his neck. His gaze heats and jacks up my pulse. "Any chance you can join me tonight?"

"I'd love to, but I don't know where you live." Why did I say it like that? All hesitant and unsure?

"It's not hard to find me, city girl." His low chuckle makes my insides flutter.

It's because he makes me nervous. Things between us are moving fast. Maybe I should pump on the brakes and take a breather?

It makes sense, but is that what I want? His warm, masculine scent floods my entire being, warming me up from the inside out. It's a message telling me to grab hold and hang on. Doesn't do anything to settle my nerves.

I want another night like last night. A movie date and what followed in the back of his truck. But I don't want all of our time together to be about sex. There's so much I want to know about him, like how he got that scar.

"Then it's a date." Drake leans down and presses his lips lightly to my cheek. "I look forward to seeing you later tonight."

With those words, Drake releases me. I slide into Sara's car and we head back to the clinic. Uncle Pete appears more tired than I anticipated, which works to my advantage.

I take over all of his appointments for the day, meeting the people who will become my future patients.

It's good to be practicing medicine again.

The afternoon is long, but I'm in heaven. When Uncle Pete and I leave the clinic, I walk on cloud nine. All my fears about stepping into the role of town doc dissipate. My confidence returns, surging within me. I won't have the years I wanted, working beside my uncle, but my practice is good.

Solid.

I can do this.

I help Uncle Pete out to his car, tired, but jazzed by a wonderful first day. When we get to his car, I can't believe my eyes.

All four tires are slashed.

21

FRIDAY

Sara gives my uncle a ride home while I wait for Henry Watkins to come by with a flatbed tow truck.

"It'll do damage if I drag it up." He walks around my uncle's car, pulling at his chin, then squats by one of the front tires, reading off the information while writing it down on a small notepad. "I think it's best if I put the car on blocks, take the tires back to my shop, put new ones on, and come back." He glances at me for approval.

I thought he'd tow the car back to his shop, take care of it there, but I suppose he can't do that with all four tires out of commission.

"Can I give you a lift?"

"That would be great, thank you." I glance at my uncle's car, not sure if it's safe to leave it.

"Can do." He stands and tugs on his jeans, pulling his pants up. Henry definitely has the ass crack thing down to a T.

As he drives me home, Henry asks about my day, but he's mostly interested in my uncle's health.

"I was able to pop by and inflate your tires. Any idea how that happened?" We pull up to my uncle's house and he turns off the engine.

"I honestly don't know."

"You were missing all four valve caps."

"My uncle mentioned the same thing when we looked at it this morning. I thought they popped off during the crash and figured that's why the air let out."

Henry scratches his ass. "They screw on to keep dirt and other debris off the valves but do nothing when it comes to keeping air in, and I checked your tires after the accident. They were all there. Someone intentionally removed them. They would've had to depress the valve inside to let the air out. It takes time to make a tire go flat that way. Whoever removed the caps was very deliberate in what they did." He gives a shake of his head. "Any reason anyone would want to mess with you?"

"Not that I can think of. Uncle Pete thought it was kids having fun."

"Could be; kids are kids. Some are good. Some are bad. But I don't think any of them would do something like that."

"Maybe it's something like picking on the new person in town?"

Henry's brows arch like that's the dumbest thing anyone could say, but it's the only thing I can think of. Nobody here knows me.

"Thank you for inflating my tires. I really appreciate it. What do I owe you?"

"Luv, you don't need to pay me for that."

"I don't want to take advantage of you."

"Trust me, you're not." Henry waves off any further talk about that.

Satisfied with his inspection, he waves goodbye and tells me he's going to head back to my uncle's car to fix everything.

I'm a bit at a loss by how much everyone helps one another.

It's cool.

With my steps light, I walk to the front door but pause at a foul stench. There's a pile of dog shit on the porch. Screwing up my nose, I step over the mess and head inside.

My uncle is asleep in his worn leather recliner. I cover him with the throw my aunt made for him then head to the kitchen to get something to clean up the mess outside.

I've heard of people not cleaning up after their dogs when on a walk, but who lets a dog loose to crap right outside the front door?

When I open the door, movement to my left catches my eye, but when I turn, there's nothing there. I clean up the dog poop and take a moment to glance up and down the street. Whoever that was, they were in the yard. Or maybe it was the dog and I chased it off?

A chill worms its way between my shoulder blades.

I double-check the door and turn the security lock for an extra degree of protection. Something about all of this feels off.

As for heading over to Drake's later tonight, I make an executive decision.

I dial Drake's number, feeling a bit deflated. The moment his deep voice hit's my ear, I almost change my mind.

"Hey, city girl." The way my nickname rolls off his tongue sends licks of heat shooting through me. "How're you doing?"

"I'm good. Someone slashed the tires of my uncle's car after lunch."

"I'll be right over." Drake's already in rescue mode. I'm not used to that.

"Thanks, but I called Henry. He's taking care of it."

"Henry's a good guy." Drake sounds troubled.

"About tonight ..." I bite my lower lip, not wanting to cancel our date, but I need a good night's rest if I'm going to tackle a full day in the clinic tomorrow.

"Are you ditching me?" He doesn't sound happy, but unlike Scott, the change in plans doesn't anger Drake.

Scott would've thrown a fit, calling me irresponsible and inconsiderate, among other more colorful names.

"I'm sorry, but I want to get to work early and help out as I can." I move around the house, tidying things up.

In the kitchen, I pause by the window to take stock of Boston.

My poor fern doesn't look too good. All the edges are black curled crisps of its former lush, green glory. I don't think Boston's going to pull through his ordeal of being left to freeze through that horrible blizzard.

My midnight stroll down the highway in the middle of that blizzard is something I'll be happy never to repeat. That bone-chilling cold nearly did me in. The wolves scared me, but I didn't have to think about that too much.

Not with Drake's sharp-shooting.

There's so much about him I don't know. He's prior military. Uncle Pete said so, but that's not where the scar came from.

"I won't pretend I wasn't hoping we could get together, but I get needing to be well-rested to see patients." Drake is easygoing compared to Scott. "How about we stick to our Friday and Saturday night plan?"

The memory of Drake pronouncing me as *his girl* gives me butterflies. That kind of possession is sexy, romantic even. It's very different from the jealousy and control Scott inflicted on me.

"I would really like that. Any chance we could meet up before then?"

"I'd love to, but I'm headed out of town tomorrow. I need to check on the cattle and will be on the ranch for a few days. I'll be back on Friday, and I promise another movie night."

"That sounds amazing. We didn't get to watch *Return of the Jedi*."

The first three *Star Wars* movies are my favorite, but I look forward to binging them all with Drake.

"It's a date then, city girl." His melodious voice tunnels straight to my core, bringing back needy sensations.

With our chemistry, I'm pretty sure we won't make it past the opening credits.

"It's a date."

When I end the call with Drake, movement in the backyard catches my eye. A loud clatter follows. Either someone's out by the woodshed, or there's a cat or a raccoon getting into stuff.

It takes a minute to find where my uncle stores his flashlight. I check the batteries and head outside, looking to scare away the cat, or raccoon, or maybe that doorstep pooping dog.

The night air carries a chilly bite to it, making me shiver and pull my shoulders to my ears. Very much unlike Redlands, it's dark outside. The city lights are so overwhelming in Redlands it's rare to see anything more than the brightest stars. In Peace Springs, there are no city lights, and the streetlights are few and far in between.

Halfway to my uncle's shed, the flashlight dies. I knock it a couple of times and it flickers on, the light noticeably dimmer than before.

The flashlight manages to stay lit long enough for me to open the door to the shed and check inside. I stand by the door, not wanting to get caught in there with a stray. A quick sweep of the light, and I see nothing concerning.

One thing about my uncle is that he's OCD neat. Everything has a place, and everything is in its place. Securely latching the shed door, I make a quick circuit of the tiny building. The lids to the trash cans are scattered on the ground.

I'm guessing it was a raccoon.

A quick circuit of the yard and nothing else appears out of place. Before I head in, I return to the trash cans and replace the lids, just in case it rains later tonight. Not that it will.

There's not a cloud in the sky. The flashlight batteries finally give up and die, but I remain in the backyard for a few more minutes, marveling at the number of stars overhead.

It's simply amazing.

I take in a deep breath and lift my face to the heavens. Peace Springs is a good place, and while I ran from Redlands, I feel as if starting over here is going to be the best thing I've ever done.

As I head inside, movement in the back of the yard spins me around. I peer into the darkness and cock my head, listening for that raccoon. I hear nothing other than the whispering of the wind.

Upon my return, my uncle isn't in the chair. I check his room and see he put himself to bed. He clutches Aunt Martha's afghan, holding it tight to his chest. The strong, powerful man from my youth is gaunt and frail, yet there's a peacefulness to his expression that warms my heart.

I don't want him to leave me, but I'm happy he'll be reunited with the love of his life. I can only hope to be as blessed as my aunt and uncle when it comes to love.

So far, my track record is pathetic. Although, things are looking up in Peace Springs.

With those thoughts running through my mind, I close up the house for the night. I check every door and every window, closing latches and double-checking the locks.

Then a pang of sorrow hits me. Someday soon, this will be my house, and I'll be all alone.

No parents.

No Aunt Marta or Uncle Pete.

No cousins.

No extended family.

Life is going to be lonely, which is a good reason to throw myself into work.

I do exactly that for the rest of the week.

The relief in Pamela and Craig's faces each day when I power through a busy morning clinic is all the reward I need. They've been seeing their patients and splitting my uncle's load for months. They deserve a vacation. I just don't know when I can give that to them.

As for me, I'm simply looking forward to tonight.

It's Friday.

Which means, I have a date, and hopefully a movie neither of us will watch.

22

MOVIE NIGHT

"TELL ME ABOUT YOUR FIRST WEEK AT WORK." DRAKE DRAWS LAZY circles on the inside of my wrist, sending sparks of electricity shooting through my nervous system with his feather-light touch.

I'm relaxed, more relaxed than I've ever been.

We're back at the farm. Or is it a ranch?

Wherever we are, it's the most romantic place on earth.

Just like last time, he ties a sheet between two trees, anchoring the bottoms to rocks on the ground to form our movie screen. Despite my thoughts on whether we'll make it through the movie, we move along nicely.

Like every boy on the planet, Drake confesses his obsession with Leia after that scene with Jabba the Hut and her skimpy outfit. It brings a smirk to my lips that stays a beat too long. I have fantasies too, but I'm not brave enough to voice them.

At least, not yet.

The Ewoks annoy me. Never understood why they had to put that in what is otherwise a fabulous ending to an amazing trilogy.

As far as our outdoor *theater* goes, it's a balmy night. A bit on the warm side, but it's a pleasant warmth rather than an oppressive heat. Give it a month or two, and it'll be almost too hot to be outdoors.

The herd is closer than the last time. Their dark-brown, soulful eyes stare at me from the other side of the barbed-wire fence.

Every now and again, they huff, blowing sharply out through their nostrils. There's silence for a bit, then one of them lets out a long, lowing sound. Others follow, until the herd says what it needs to say.

Overhead, a heavy dusting of stars fills the heavens. Without the light of the moon to wash out millions of stars, the Milky Way takes center stage. I understand why that swath of stars earned its name.

It's majestic.

"Where are we?" My fingers twine with Drake's as I take another sip of wine.

Drake copies me, only he drinks whiskey rather than wine. We disagree on which is better.

"We're right where we're supposed to be." His warm dark eyes are pools of simmering desire. Although, he seems to be in no hurry to move things along.

Last time, we had a fire and he cooked steaks. Something I don't think the cows behind us knew about at the time. Today, we dine on smoked salmon, cream cheese, crackers, and other finger foods.

"You know what I mean, silly." I playfully punch his arm.

I've learned not to hit him hard. The man is a solid wall of muscle. Hitting him is like slamming my fist against granite.

"Do I?"

"Is this your land? Or Bert's?"

It could belong to the Bureau of Land Management with free, public access to all. There are millions of acres of public land in California. I assume the same goes for Montana.

Unlike last time, there's no blindfold and no assist from Bert setting up our spot for the night.

"Did you recognize anything from the drive up?" Drake turns to me, eyes simmering with banked heat.

Without the blindfold, I enjoyed the drive more than I thought possible. Something about the rolling plains settles in like a long-lost friend. This place feels like home.

"Not really." I bring his hand to my lips and flutter my lips over his knuckles. "Did you know I have land up here?"

"City girl, everyone knows that." His brows pinch together, confused. Not the expression I expect.

"They do?"

"Of course. You're the last McPhearson woman, with thousands of acres under your care."

"I didn't realize it was common knowledge."

"Remind me to take you to the Town Hall. I think you're going to enjoy it."

"Really? Why's that?"

"Your family is a local legend. That's all I'm going to say for now."

"Is that good or bad?"

Legend?

There's definitely a story there.

"It's good. Strong. Resilient. Charitable." He winks at me. "Not to mention how much that land means to those who farm it and run cattle on it."

"I need to figure out what to do with it."

"Do with it?" He shifts in his seat. "What do you mean?"

"I think I should sell it."

"You're kidding, right?" He leans back and folds his arms across his chest. His dark brows knit together, concerned and confused.

"I don't know what I'm going to do with it. It's a lot to deal with."

"Before you make any decisions, you should talk to the manager."

"The manager?"

"Yeah, the guy hired to take care of the land." He shifts away from me, almost as if my words wound him.

"That's a good idea. I'll talk to my uncle about setting up a meeting. Although, I have to tell you, I'm nervous about what it entails."

"How's that?"

"I know nothing about land management."

"I'm sure the manager has that all figured out." There's a look in his face I can't figure out, almost as if Drake's having fun with me.

"No doubt. I'm overwhelmed enough settling in with the day job.

Adding the management of ten thousand acres? I think my head is going to explode. How will I know what he tells me is the truth? I'm so afraid of being taken advantage of."

"Don't be." Again, I sense something. "No one is going to take advantage of you, and you'll get nothing but the honest truth from the manager."

"How do you know that?" I'm overwhelmed.

I knew moving to Peace Springs would be challenging. I know nothing about owning a medical practice. I was an employee at the place I worked at before. I went to work. Saw my patients. Went home. The next day I did it all over again. I didn't have to worry about billing, scheduling, payroll, malpractice insurance, or any of the other things I don't know.

"You're smart as a tack, city girl. You'll figure it all out."

"What scares me isn't what I don't know."

"That so?" His brows tug together, concerned and worried.

The way he cares about me comes as a shock. More so, because I'm not used to it. Scott never cared about what bothered me. I had to deal with that all on my own.

Drake cares.

More than cares.

He's deeply invested in me.

I would try to explain where I'm coming from, but that's impossible. How is he going to understand the pressure I'm under?

"Here's my problem."

"Go on, city girl."

"I'm not afraid of what I don't know." I begin with the obvious. "It's a long list, but I'm willing to learn. It's the things I don't know that I don't know that worry me."

"Wait a second ..." Drake leans back, pulling at his chin. "The things you don't know that you don't know?"

"Exactly. Those things will slip through the cracks, and I won't even be aware of it."

"I can see how that could be troubling, but you don't need to worry."

"How can you be so sure?"

"I know Sara. She's tenacious and OCD when it comes to the business. Your uncle set you up for success. He surrounded you with quality people. Good people. Honest and hardworking people. And I know the guy who manages your land."

"You do?"

"Yes, Abby, I do." There's an odd twinkle in his eye. He cocks his head, as if waiting for me to say something, but then he shakes his head. "Luv, I manage the McPhearson land."

"Wait a second." My jaw literally drops. "You're the manager?"

"Have been for years. It made sense when your aunt first got sick. My homestead abuts McPhearson property. Your aunt hired me to take care of the land until you came into your inheritance and could take over."

"Take over. I have zero experience managing land."

"I can teach you everything you need to know."

"Did you not hear me when I said my brain's going to explode?" I tilt my head back and stare at the stars overhead. "I'm so out of my element."

I know enough about medicine to guess at what else is involved in managing a thriving medical practice, but land? I'm clueless as to what I need to worry about.

But I have Drake.

Why didn't Uncle Pete mention that when he told me about the McPhearson land? Kind of an odd thing to leave out.

"My uncle didn't tell me you managed the land."

"I'm not surprised by that."

"Really? Why?"

"He knows you have a lot on your plate, but I'm here to teach you everything you need to know."

"I appreciate that."

"How are you handling his illness?"

"It's tough."

Drake takes my hand. The warmth of his fingers wrapping around my hand comforts me.

"When I found out, I didn't know what to think, but after talking to him and watching him, I can tell he's tired. He's ready to move on."

"Ah, luv." Drake pulls me into his arms, kissing the top of my head. "I know we're still getting to know each other, but I'm here if you need a shoulder to cry on."

"Thank you, but I need your brain more."

"My brain?"

"It's a relief to know you're the manager for McPhearson lands. I don't know where to begin. Who are the tenet farmers? The ranchers who lease the pastureland? What agreements are in place? Do they pay rent? I don't even know the right terms to use when framing my questions. I'm certain *rent* is the wrong word. Not to mention, I don't remember where that land is."

"Slow down, city girl, and take a breath." He grasps both my hands and forces me to stare into his mesmerizing eyes.

There's strength there. Comfort. Control. And a willingness to help.

"I must be the biggest joke in town."

"Why would you say that?"

"I inherit ten thousand acres and I don't know where that land is." I shake my head and vent a frustrated sigh. One more thing to add to my to-do list.

Drake stares back at me, then the corners of his mouth twitch. From the mirth in his eyes, he barely holds back from laughing.

At me.

I watch his efforts slowly fail as he tries to keep a straight face, but it's a complete loss. Drake finally breaks and laughs his head off. I can't help but smile. He laughs with the entirety of his being.

It's infectious and I join in, laughing at the silliness of a landowner who doesn't know where her land is located. Over-whelmed doesn't touch on how I'm feeling about all of this, but the best medicine truly is laughter.

Sure, I spent my summers playing in the streams and rivers on that land, but I was a kid. I never paid attention *where* we drove to get to our picnic place.

"You think too hard, city girl." Drake's laughter dies down as he pulls me into his lap. His touch brings me back to the present as he wraps me in his protective embrace. "We'll figure all of it out together. Is that okay?"

Okay? It's more than okay. I trust Drake, which means it's easy to extend that trust to helping me take care of ten thousand acres.

"Sorry. I'm stressed."

"Come." Drake lifts me off his lap.

He stands, then offers me his hand. I take it, feeling comforted by his touch as he leads me to the fence line where a dozen cattle on the other side chomp contentedly on the grass. Or are they chewing their cud?

Is that the right word?

I'm so *not* a farm girl.

"Look." He stretches his hand while one of the cows closes in to nuzzle his palm. After they say hello, Drake rubs the side of the cow's face.

"They scare me." I step back, staying out of reach.

"No need to be scared." Drake takes my hand, pulling me forward. He lifts our joined hands up to the cow's face. There he places my palm alongside the cow's muzzle.

The hair is softer than I thought it would be. The cow flicks its ears and the tag punched into its ear flaps. The cow snorts, which makes me yank back my hand in surprise.

Drake gives a soft laugh and guides my hand back up to the cow's face. I stroke it from cheek to nostril and back again.

"They're gentle creatures. Nothing to be afraid of." Drake's voice resonates deep in my chest, settling in and making itself at home. "This fence line is the boundary between my land and yours." He points to the cattle. "They belong to one of your tenet ranchers. We'll find time to introduce you to everyone. Your uncle asked me to wait until you got settled with the medical practice before overwhelming you with all of this."

"Thank you." And I mean that in the most honest and basic way possible.

Things no longer feel as overwhelming as they did a few moments ago. I've got good people working with me, helping me. I no longer feel so alone. Off in the distance, the long howl of a wolf pierces the air. Drake stiffens beside me.

"I didn't realize how much of a nuisance they've become," I admit my lack of knowledge.

After my wolf encounter, I looked up everything I could regarding wolves. Turns out Drake is right about them no longer being endangered. With a permit, he's able to cull up to a hundred wolves a year from his lands.

I'm simply a softie at heart. I don't want the wolves killed, but I don't want one of these gentle cows taken down either.

Or one of Bert's llamas.

We stay with the cows while the Empire falls and the Rebels prevail. The projector cuts out, plunging us into near-total darkness. Drake and I don't move, silently, absorbing the moment while we do nothing other than stand side-by-side.

Drake grabs my hand and leads me back to his truck.

"Drake ..."

"Yes, luv?"

"Can I ask you a question?"

"Sure thing, city girl."

In the darkness, the ragged scar on his face is hard to see. I need to know more about the man standing beside me.

He walks us around to the back of the truck where the tailgate is down. Before I know what's happening, he grasps my waist and lifts me up onto the tailgate. He jumps up to sit beside me. Like last time, blankets spread across the truck bed.

Tonight, however, feels different. Instead of a fuckfest we take things slow. Which is good. It lets me ask about something I'm curious about.

"Will you tell me about your scar?"

23

SCAR

DRAKE'S ENTIRE DEMEANOR CHANGES WITHIN THE SPAN OF A heartbeat. His body stiffens. He drops my hand as if stung. Most damning of all is the slight shifting away from me.

"I'm sorry." I hold up a hand, feeling as if I've made a terrible mistake. "You don't have to tell me if you don't want to."

Drake turns away. His shoulders hunch, and he draws into himself.

I stretch out a hand, but pull back, afraid to touch him. This is what I was afraid of, me pushing when I should just shut the fuck up.

He takes in a deep breath and then another. His head tilts back until he stares at the stars. I remember doing exactly the same thing not too long ago.

I don't dare breathe; too afraid I made a horrible mistake.

We sit in silence for a moment while I rub my hands against my jeans, needing to do something. I'm about ready to jump down to the ground when his entire body relaxes.

"It was a long time ago."

"I shouldn't have said anything. I'm sorry."

"It's okay. I don't want any secrets between us. Katie was a big part of my life."

"Katie?"

"My wife."

His wife?

A fist tightens around my throat, choking me while my heart takes a nosedive, plummeting so fast that I can't help but tremble.

He's married?

Too terrified to ask anything else, I try to still the trembling of my body. I swallow a few times, trying to reopen my throat and force a few words out. I finally manage the impossible feat.

"I didn't know you're married." My voice is tight and unsure.

Wounded.

If he's married, why the hell is he out here with me? How could he fuck me if he's married to another woman?

I don't know whether to be hurt, enraged, or something else. It's as if my mind *stops* and finds itself incapable of processing any other thoughts.

Drake turns toward me. When he speaks, an aching loneliness fills his voice. "I *was* married." He takes my hand in his and gives a little tug. "Abby, look at me."

I would, except I don't want him to see the tears tumbling down my cheeks.

Drake hops off the tailgate and spins around to face me. He places his hands on my knees, and with gentle pressure, forces my knees apart. He wedges himself between my legs, then he grabs my upper arms and gives me a little shake.

"I read you like an open book, city girl, and that thing going on in your head is not what this is."

"What's going on in my head?"

"You think I'm cheating on my wife, messing around with you."

Damn, he *can* read me like an open book.

"Let me fill in some of the details and answer your question." He releases my arms and takes the pad of his thumb to wipe away my tears.

"I was married to Katie. Past tense."

"I'm sorry. I jumped to conclusions." I scrub away my tears.

"I saw that, and I have to wonder why." His head cocks to the side. Thoughts churn behind his eyes. "Did someone hurt you?"

In more ways than one, but I don't answer. I can't. Not without opening up a can of worms about Scott.

Intensely jealous, if I looked at another man for any reason, Scott took his anger out on me. I learned not to give Scott any ammunition to use against me. Each of my visits to an emergency room came after such an event. I used to keep count, but then I stopped.

Drake seems to take my silence for what it is: me not wanting to dive down that rabbit hole. I wet my lips and swallow past the lump in my throat.

"What happened with Katie?"

"An unfortunate series of events." His posture changes, tightening for a second, vibrating with rage, and then suddenly relaxing again. "It's how I got the scar."

"I thought you might have gotten it in the military. My uncle said you're ex-military."

"I am, which is where the unfortunate part of the story comes in."

"You don't have to tell me if you don't want to."

"Honestly, I don't like thinking about it, but I want you to know. Heck, I want you to know everything about me." His stony expression cracks and a boyish grin lights up his face.

I wait for him to continue, letting him tell me at his own pace. Storm clouds churn in the darkness of his eyes as flashes of anger reveal something else. I don't know what Drake did in the military, but I have a sinking suspicion I can guess at it.

"I married Katie when we were young, before I went into the military. We tried really hard to have kids, but deployments and the stress of my job made that challenging. Within a few months of getting out, Katie got pregnant. We were so excited."

I place my hand on his arm, knowing his story doesn't end well. My gut churns and my chest tightens in anticipation of what he's going to say. I already know I don't want to hear about his pain, but there's no way around it now.

"She wanted to surprise her parents in person, so we packed up the car and headed to Oklahoma. We were strapped for time and cash. I pushed through the night, hoping to make it in one day. We didn't have enough money to get a hotel room. When I pulled into a gas station to fill up, I wasn't thinking. Which isn't like me. I'm trained to be aware of my surroundings at all times, but I let my guard down. Like Katie, I was excited."

My grip on his arm tightens as pain fills his expression.

"Katie got out of the car. She needed to use the restroom. That's when the men attacked."

"Oh, Drake ..." I definitely don't want to know the end of this story.

"When they grabbed her, I reacted, doing what I was trained to do. I took them out one by one. Only the third man had a knife and a hold of Katie. I rushed him when I realized what he was about to do. He slashed her throat and then my face."

"Oh, Drake." My heart breaks for him. "I didn't mean to make you relive that."

"It's been several years. Some days, it's surreal. Other days, it hurts. Bert's been telling me it's time to move on for years now. You should've heard him go on and on the night I brought you to his house."

"I had no idea." I cup the side of his face.

"Katie died and took our unborn baby with her. The three men didn't make it. There was an investigation, but fortunately, it was all caught on tape, and that's the story about my scar."

He wears the constant reminder of his wife and unborn child's death, on his face. At a loss for words, I cup his face. Leaning in, I kiss him softly.

Gently.

Drake holds perfectly still, then leans into my touch. Taking my hand, he slowly draws my fingers over the long gash which marks him from the corner of his eye to the corner of his mouth.

The scar tissue is tough, rubbery compared to the skin of his face, and heartbreaking. I break off the kiss and we do nothing other than simply stare at each other for several long moments.

Then, he suddenly shifts gears.

"There's supposed to be a meteor shower tonight. What do you think about looking for shooting stars?" He climbs back into the truck, smoothing out the blankets and punching the pillows.

I join him, scooting beside him, then lie down. His fingers curl with mine as we watch the heavens and try to forget the past.

He shared what must've been the worst moment of his life while I still hold onto a secret of my own. It was hard enough to open up to my uncle about the abuse, and I'm not happy with why I felt comfortable telling him. A part of me knows he won't be around long. My secret will die with him.

I'm ashamed of that part of my past. Wracked with guilt that I, a smart woman, fell victim to abuse. I never understood why women stayed with their abusers, and it took me far too long to realize I became one of them.

But there's fear, and then there's *fear*.

No one can understand the terror I lived with day in and day out.

I must have fallen asleep because the next thing I know, there's a snort and a huff right by my ear. It smells like half-digested grass.

Pungent comes to mind.

My lids open and it takes a second before I focus. The hot breath of a cow chewing its cud brings a toe-curling scream to my lips. Its placid gaze takes me in as it flaps its ears, making the tag in its ear flutter.

Then I realize the truck is surrounded by cows. Dozens and dozens of heifers surround Drake's truck.

"What the fuck?" Drake wakes beside me and stares at the herd in confusion. "How the hell did they get here?"

"Are you asking me?" I point to my chest as Drake jumps out of the back of the truck. He lands right between two of the heifers and places his hands on his hips. "Need a hand down?"

I look at him as if he's a crazy man.

"There's no way in hell I'm getting out of this truck."

"They're not going to hurt you."

"I'm perfectly fine where I am."

I don't care what Drake says. There's no way I'm jumping down into a herd of cattle. I don't care that he says that they won't hurt me. My brain is screaming that they'll trample me.

Drake scratches his head and pushes cows out of the way as he stomps to the fence. I stand in the back of the truck peering over the cows as he picks up what looks like an end of a piece of barbed wire. He glances at the ground, moving between the posts.

"What is it?" I strain to see what he's doing.

"Someone cut the fence." He turns back to the cows. "That's how they got out."

Drake marches back to the truck. He pushes a cow away from the passenger door and leans inside, where he grabs his cellphone.

I stay in the back of the truck as Drake makes several calls. He finally shoves the phone into his back pocket and looks around.

"What do we do now?" This is so far outside my wheelhouse, I feel completely useless.

"We round up the cows, get them back on the other side of the fence and wait for help."

"Help?"

"Yeah, we've got to mend that fence."

"How did it break? Did the cows do that?"

He looks at me like I'm an idiot. "Cows stay well away from barbed wire. They didn't do this. Someone else did."

"What does that mean?" An unsettled feeling overcomes me. There was nothing wrong with that fence last night. Which means ...

"Someone cut it while we were sleeping." Drake's brows tug together as his expression darkens. He walks up and down the gap in the fence, looking for something.

All I see is churned earth, turned over from the hooves of the cows. I know what he's looking for. Drake's looking for signs of who might have done this.

My hand flies to my belly as the butterflies take flight. Unlike before, that's not a rush of excitement, but rather fear.

I hope to God whoever did this isn't who I think it is.

24

HURT

LESS THAN AN HOUR LATER, WE'RE JOINED BY FIVE MEN WHO PILE OUT OF several beat-up pickup trucks. In jeans, cowboy boots, and the requisite cowboy hat, the men fit my image of *ranch hand* to a T.

It takes them less than a minute to get to work. One of them brings an Australian Shepard who's more than eager to round up the cows. Two of them inspect the fence with Drake, while the last two yank tools out of the back of one of the trucks.

It's amazing watching the men work, but even more fascinating is the dog.

It took well over twenty minutes for Drake to get four of the cattle back onto the other side of the busted fence while we waited for reinforcements. When he went back for a fifth, two of the cows followed him, rejoining the herd on the wrong side of the fence.

The dog doesn't have that problem. It's totally in control and loving every bit of it. I might be terrified of getting in the mix with the massive beasts, but the dog doesn't mind at all. It runs around, snapping at their hooves, getting them gathered together, then the dog magically herds the cows back through the opening like it's nothing.

They're now on the correct side of the fence, happily chewing their cud and grazing on fresh shoots of grass while the dog plops down and rests its muzzle on its paws.

With the dog done, the men get busy.

For the most part, they work in silence. Each of them knows exactly what to do, leading me to believe this isn't the first time they've worked as a team.

After a while, the men finish. Wiping the sweat from their brows, they gather together to inspect their handiwork.

I look at the ground. Last night it was thick grass. Now, it's churned mud. Unlike the men, I'm not wearing boots, and I'm not sure how much of that mud isn't excrement from the cows.

Drake appears satisfied with the fence. He makes quick introductions, but it's obvious he's eager to be alone with me again.

After a few waves, the men depart, and Drake comes to my side of the truck.

"You need some help?" He glances at the ground and then at my pathetic footwear.

"There's no way I'm stepping in any of that."

"Come here, city girl." He gestures for me to come to his side of the truck. Drake pops open the passenger door and holds his arms out.

"You're nothing short of amazing." I'm a strong, independent woman, but there's a time and a place for that.

I'm perfectly happy letting Drake play gallant hero. I climb into his arms and clutch his neck as he lifts me free of the truck bed and deposits me gently on the passenger seat.

He gives a slow shake of his head, laughing under his breath and mutters something about city girls as he circles around the truck. He jumps in and we're off.

"Wanna see some of your land?" I love the way his left eyebrow arches when he asks a question. It's sexy as sin.

As for seeing some of *my* land, it's still early, and I have nowhere to be until the clinic opens on Monday.

"I'd love to, if that's okay."

"Okay?" He gives me a look. "You realize you're technically my boss."

"Actually, I'm not your boss yet."

"How so?"

"My uncle says the trust holds the land until I turn thirty, and I'm a couple of years shy of that."

"Well ..." He taps the steering wheel with his fingers. "Then I'll do my best to keep it in trust for you." He points out the window. "We're headed north, away from town. I have five thousand acres, which I use for my cattle. Your land extends north from mine crossing out of Peace Springs and heading into Bear Creek."

"Bear Creek?"

"Small town in the mountains. I grew up there."

"I like the name. Sounds homey."

"If you think Peace Springs is small, you've seen nothing yet. Bear Creek is tiny in comparison. I'll take you there sometime."

"I'd like that." I settle into my seat, getting comfortable, as Drake heads back onto the road.

For the next couple of hours, Drake takes me on a tour of my land. When he brings me to the creek I remember as a girl, I get excited.

"Stop. Stop!"

"Here?"

"Yes, this is where my mom and my aunt used to bring me."

Drake pulls off the dusty road. I hastily unbuckle and jump out of the truck before it comes to a complete stop.

"I wish I had my bathing suit," I call over my shoulder as I race to the edge of the best swimming hole on the planet. A deep breath in brings a flood of memories racing through me.

"Why?"

"This is where I swam as a kid. My mom and my aunt brought me up here for picnics all the time."

The place looks exactly like I remember, except the shade tree we used to eat under is much larger. The water, however, is exactly the same. It flows crystal clear, tumbling over a small ledge of rock less than ten-feet high to spill into a broad pool before flowing out the other side.

Large boulders pepper the land, none taller than a man. Some are right on the edge of the swimming hole; great places to jump into the water. Others are under the water, which makes diving and jumping treacherous, but I have a few favorite rocks, cleared by my parents, as safe for jumping.

I'd leap into the air, wishing I could fly. I'd hang suspended for a fraction of a second before plummeting downward.

The water is snowmelt, which flows down from the mountains. It's crystal clear with a blueish glow and splashes into a basin carved out of the ground at the bottom of the waterfall.

All the best memories in my life happened here.

Long, lazy summer days with nothing to do, nowhere to be, and all day long to have fun. My mom and my aunt would sit on the rocks along the side, dangling their feet in the water as they read their favorite books. I swam and jumped and dove and had the best time as my fingers and toes turned to prunes from the water.

We'd take a break for lunch, and I spent an agonizing half an hour on land until my mom would let me swim again. I spent that time combing the water's edge looking for turtles, frogs, salamanders, and tiny fish hiding in the shallows. Years of memories rush through me—happier times when nothing could hurt me.

Children are truly blessed. It's only when we grow old that the world loses some of that luster.

Aunts get cancer and die. Terrible accidents steal those closest to you. Boyfriends turn violent, kicking and hitting and terrorizing those they're supposed to love.

And when you feel like things can't get any worse, the world gives you something to treasure.

Returning to Peace Springs makes me believe it truly is possible to escape Scott's brutality.

"This is a beautiful place." Drake joins me by the water's edge.

So caught up in my memories, I forget I'm not alone. Drake's steadying presence makes me reach for his arm. I wrap my hand around his bicep, thankful for the blessings Peace Springs brought me in years past and now, in the present.

"I loved coming up here."

"Tell me about it."

"My mom and aunt would bring me. We spent all day swimming and hiking and reading and playing silly games. On the weekends, Uncle Pete and my dad would join us. They made everything an adventure. We'd camp, stay up late, and stare at the stars until we all fell asleep." I tip my head back, loving the way the warmth of the sun heats my face. "We'd look for shooting stars, chase fireflies, listen to the cattle lowing in the distance. It was wonderful."

"It sounds amazing. Maybe we should move movie night and have it here instead of at my place? We can watch our favorite films, do a little skinny dipping, cuddle to get warm ..." His voice trails off and I know exactly what he's thinking.

There's more water spilling over the rocky ledge than I remember. The creek leading out is a bit wider than I recall. Other than that, it's picture-perfect.

"You love this place." He meanders toward the creek leading away from the swimming hole. There, he dips his muddy boots into the clear water, letting the gentle flow clean off the mud clinging to his boots. He glances over his shoulder and a mischievous glint sparkles in his eyes. "I'm thinking a little skinny dipping might be fun." Before I know it, he kicks off his boots and yanks off his shirt.

"Last one in is a rotten egg!" He fumbles with his belt buckle while I race to the water's edge.

That water is cold, cold, cold. I definitely remember how cold it was, and most surely still is, but I don't care. A sense of being carefree overcomes me, and there's no way I'm losing that bet.

Following Drake's lead, I yank my shirt over my head and kick off my shoes while undoing my bra. My thumbs hook in my panties and I yank them off. I stop by Drake, who's still having problems with his jeans.

With kid-like glee, I snap my panties at him and laugh as they hit his face. Drake doesn't miss a beat. He grabs my panties and makes a show of sniffing them, then finally gets one leg free. He hops on one foot, yanking his jeans off while still holding my panties to his face. He runs behind me in his boxer briefs.

"That's not fair." He closes the distance between us as I race toward my favorite rock. The water here is deep, and I spent my summers jumping off that rock. I know it's safe to launch into the air and let gravity take over.

I do that now, running without a care in the world and leap off the edge. It's the only way to deal with the chilly water. There is no going slow.

For a split second, I'm in the air. Then I drop, gasping as the bone-chilling waters shock my body. I press my lips tight together and pinch my eyes as the water closes over my head.

Way colder than I remember as a girl, I'm not prepared for the icy shock of the frigid waters. I claw my way to the surface, shivering and turning blue. Drake stands above me, still on the rock, my red lace panties gripped in his hand.

"No way did I think you'd do that." He shakes his head, laughs, then jumps in, tucking knees to chest, and cannonballs me.

Icy water sprays my face as I kick to shore. I think I'm going to make it when a firm hand grabs my ankle. Drake yanks hard, pulling me back. My head goes under.

It's cold. Like colder than the night we met when I battled frost-bite and won. Already, my body grows sluggish, but then Drake's arm locks around me and our legs intertwine as we tread water. He brushes the hair off my face and stares deeply into my eyes.

"You are something else, city girl. An unexpected treasure."

With those words, he kisses me. It would be way more romantic if I could feel my lips, but I'll take every kiss he wants to give me. I thread my fingers into the hair at his nape, loving the silky glide of his wet hair and shiver.

"I-I th-think we should get out of the water."

"Agree." Drake releases me and we both angle toward the shore.

His long strokes get him there before me, which means I get to watch the water sluicing off his naked body.

Damn, but the man has a nice ass.

He turns around, one hand cupping his groin, and extends a hand out to me. I take his hand and find my footing. His gaze drops to my chest, where my nipples are cold, hard pebbles.

"Don't even think it." I wade out of the water, flapping my arms like a chicken as I try to get my blood circulating. Thankfully, the sun's up far enough to heat the air.

Immediately, sensation rushes back to my toes, my fingers, and my kneecaps. Who knew kneecaps could get cold like that?

"I don't remember it being that cold when I was a kid."

"I'm not surprised, but it's a month earlier than when you came up."

I pause and decide he's right. "Come to think of it, we came up in mid-June and left mid-August."

"That water's probably not even forty degrees."

"It certainly felt like diving into an ice bath." I gather my hair, wringing it to get as much water out as possible. As for my clothes, they're strewn about.

I gather everything and walk back to his truck naked. Drake follows me, getting closer.

Closer still.

I feel him all around me, and my heart rate spikes.

The man has an effect on me.

Combine that with the fact we're both naked and the inevitable is bound to happen.

Spinning around, he brackets me between his rock-hard body and the metal of the truck. Normally, I wouldn't lean against a work truck, but the hood is warm, radiating the engine's heat.

Drake stares at me, desire smoldering in his eyes. Strings of dark hair cling to his face. The scar is whiter than I remember, probably a result of the cold.

"I know one way to get warm." His heated gaze simmers.

"Really?"

"Want me to show you?"

"Yes, please."

No way I'm saying no to that.

With my heart pounding in my throat, the tonal undertones of his voice melt me from the inside out. His sheer size blocks my escape, not that I'm interested in escaping him.

Despite the scar, his face is unbearably handsome, marred for life by the most unfortunate of accidents. We're both drenched but drying fast. His masculine aroma hits my nose, flooding my senses with his need.

Drake's hand closes around my throat. It's meant to be sensual, sexy, but blood pounds in my ears, and my pulse skyrockets. My breaths turn spastic. Hyperventilating, blood roars past my ears as memories of a different man fill my mind.

Scott used to choke me when he beat me, cutting off my air until I passed out. He would do it over and over again, brutally punishing me for whatever mistake I had made.

My vision swims, and my legs buckle.

The world tilts beneath me as I crumble.

"Abby!" Drake's shout sounds a mile away.

I'm being carried. His bare feet slap against the firm ground. He jostles me as something solid, something metal, falls and then stops. Cold metal presses against my bare skin as I blink and the world comes back into focus.

Drake peers at me, leaning in, staring at each of my eyes in turn. He presses the pads of his fingers against my inner wrist, feeling for a pulse.

He's going to feel the panic swimming in my veins.

I blink again and take a deep breath. Some of the constriction around my chest eases.

"What happened?" Drake lifts my chin and forces me to look at him.

His brows tug together. Ex-military, he knows a post-traumatic episode when he sees one. There's no way I'm getting away with not telling him.

I wipe at my cheeks and take in a deep breath.

"Who hurt you?" He barely touches my throat.

I sniff and straighten my spine. If he had the strength to tell me about his scar, and losing his wife along with their unborn child, then I can tell him about Scott.

"It's not your fault." I don't want him to be afraid to touch me. "That's just something ..." My voice trails off. This is harder than I think it should be.

"That triggers you?" He takes half a step back. "Who hurt you?"

I take in a deep breath. "Moving here gave me the excuse I needed to get out of Redlands."

"Get out? Or get away?"

"Both." I hang my head in shame and tell him about Scott.

He doesn't interrupt, letting me tell him at my own pace.

I cry.

I get angry.

I berate myself. That's when he touches me, calming me down.

When I run out of words, Drake draws me into his embrace.

"You're safe, Abby. No one will ever hurt you again." He states it like a promise; a promise I know he'll keep.

Scott's a thousand miles in my rearview mirror. I'm free of his abuse. With my freak-out episode killing the mood, Drake and I dress in silence. He comes to me, pulls me into his arms, and does nothing other than hold me for what seems like forever.

In his arms, I feel safe.

In his arms, I feel his pain.

In his arms, we hold the trauma of our pasts, and it suddenly feels like less of a burden.

I'm no longer alone.

We pile into his truck and head back to town, saying little as the miles fall behind us.

The rest of the day, we goof off, winding up at Eddie's Soda Shoppe, where we gorge on burgers, milkshakes, and fries. He takes me to Top Bar, where I order a glass of wine and he, of course, orders a whiskey. Neat.

With liquid courage flowing in my veins, somehow, he convinces me to join the crowd on the dance floor.

It takes a minute to learn the steps of the line dance, but before I know it, I'm laughing and dancing and having the best time of my life.

But all good things come to an end.

25

HOME

IT'S NEARLY MIDNIGHT WHEN DRAKE DROPS ME OFF AT MY HOUSE. HE kisses me lightly on the lips. I invite him in, but he declines. He's uncomfortable spending the night knowing my uncle sleeps just down the hall.

I get it.

And I'm okay to wait.

Today's been a heavy day. Last night was a heavy night. We opened up to each other, sharing the pain of our pasts. We're closer for it, but I sense he needs a bit of breathing space to internalize what it all means.

I know I do.

My step is light, heart pulsating with everything that comes with falling in love.

Falling in love.

It hits me. I'm hopelessly, head over heels in love.

My uncle must've gone to bed early. All the lights are off. I head into the kitchen, tiptoeing, as I don't want to wake my uncle. As his disease progresses, fatigue pulls at him. He needs all the rest he can get.

Entering the kitchen, I catch something underfoot, kicking it across the floor. Sounding like broken glass, it skitters across the linoleum floor. I fumble for the light switch and flick on the light.

My eyes pinch when I see poor Boston on the floor, his pot shattered, blackened fronds crumbling, and roots sticking up.

Boston was on the window ledge—my attempt at resuscitating the poor fern. I've been diligently watering him. I take him outside each morning to soak up sunlight and bring him in at night, afraid we might have another freak cold snap that would doom him for good.

He's not thriving. He's barely surviving.

But I distinctly remember bringing him inside before my date with Drake last night. How the hell did he get all the way over here? If he fell off the window ledge, he'd be on the counter, or in the sink.

It's almost as if someone grabbed him and threw him on the …

I clutch at my belly as a sudden creeping sense of dread overcomes me. There's no way my uncle would touch Boston. He knows what the poor fern means to me. How important it is that Boston survive.

I suck in a breath when movement in my peripheral vision catches my eye. I turn around slowly, barely daring to move, as terror flows through my veins. The door to the pantry stands open. Leaning against the doorjamb, Scott levies a murderous gaze in my direction.

"About time you got home." He inspects his cuticles. It's a slow, agonizing movement, as if he's got all the time in the world.

I've seen him like this before. It's what he does when he decides I need to be punished. He likes to draw out the suspense, making me shake with fear.

"What are you doing here?" My fingers claw at the fabric of my shirt as I debate what to do next.

I'm too far from the kitchen door leading outside. I'm equally far from the front door. No matter which way I jump, Scott will be on me before I can escape.

I suddenly regret Drake not wanting to stay.

"The better question is why you weren't here." Malevolence boils in his gaze. Fury bunches in his shoulders. Anger flexes in his biceps. His fingers curl, forming hands into fists.

Fists I know all too well.

I gulp and slowly slide my left foot back.

At least I know what happened to poor Boston.

Scott broke in, either late last night or earlier today. No doubt he recognized the fern. In his rage, I clearly see Scott grabbing Boston, lifting the poor thing in the air, then slamming it down on the floor.

Destroying the things I care about is exactly how he operates.

Then it hits me.

"What did you do to my uncle?"

"I haven't done shit to him." Spittle flies out of Scott's mouth as he spits out the words. "He's been in his room for hours." Scott's voice rises in pitch, turning into a blood-chilling shout.

"Please ..." I hold out my hand, palm out, as if that will stop Scott.

"Hours!" Scott takes a step forward as I take one back. "Were you fucking him? Is that what you were doing?"

I could try to escape, but if my uncle is here, and I have no reason to think he isn't, there's no way I'm leaving him with Scott.

I've seen Scott mad. I've seen him angry. What I've never seen is Scott enraged. I need to get Scott outside and away from my uncle.

"We should talk outside." My voice shakes with the fear flooding my system. My legs shake like wet noodles. My breaths catch in my throat.

"Damn straight, we need to talk." He takes another step, testing me.

I've learned not to run. It was one of my earliest lessons, one beaten into me until I curled into the fetal position and begged Scott to stop hitting me until I lost my voice.

Scott hates when I force him to come after me. He thinks I should fall to my knees and beg for forgiveness he'll never give.

"Scott ..." I continue to hold out my hand as if that will stop him.

But with each word, I take another step back, drawing Scott out of the kitchen while moving me closer to the door.

If I can get out, maybe one of the neighbors will hear me scream. Maybe they'll call the cops or come running with their shotguns.

Everyone is armed. Back in Redlands, that's something I would find concerning. In Peace Springs, it's commonplace.

I gain another two feet, drawing Scott into the living room.

"Who the fuck were you with?" Scott plants his feet and looks down the hall leading to my uncle's bedroom.

"Scott ..." My voice waivers.

My gut tells me to lie. That I wasn't out with anyone, but Scott will know the lie on my tongue.

Besides, I'm positive he heard Drake and I say our goodbyes on the porch. I'm certain he saw everything.

If he's been here for hours, he watched Drake's truck pull up to the curb. He saw Drake give me a hand out of the truck. He noticed the way our fingers twined together as we held hands walking to the front door.

"You need to leave." I try rolling my shoulders back and stiffening my spine. Interjecting strength into my position, however, does nothing.

"You're coming with me." Scott glances around the living room, weighing options, finding weapons to beat me with.

His eyes glaze over with his inebriation. His emotions magnify, turning his anger into something deadly.

Too many times, this man made me fear for my life. Too many times, he decided to beat some sense into me. Too many times, I wound up in the emergency room.

My injuries included cracked ribs, concussions, abdominal bruising, black eyes, and one orbital rim fracture. All courtesy of Scott's fists.

My hand drifts up to the old injury as the memory of that night returns. I slide my right foot back.

"Don't." His low growl freezes me in my tracks. "Don't you dare run from me."

26

STALKER

"You need to leave." Again, I try to inject strength into my voice.

Once more, I fail.

"Oh, I'm going to leave." Scott takes two menacing steps toward me. "And you're coming with me."

I back away.

He rushes me, closing the distance. Fingers digging into my arm with punishing force, Scott grabs me.

I instinctively jerk, trying to free myself. He clamps down and pulls me off my feet. I slam into him and bounce off his hard chest.

"Abby?" My uncle's frail voice sounds from his room at the far end of the hall.

"Let me go!" I pry at Scott's fingers, but it does nothing.

Scott grabs me by the throat and slams my back against the front door. The wood rattles. The windows shudder. His grip tightens. I gasp, clutching at his fingers with my free hand.

Scott leans in. His features draw back as fury builds in his gaze.

"You. Belong. To. Me." He crushes his lips against mine. Forcing me to bear a kiss I don't want.

"Abby?" My uncle's voice sounds closer, and that's when I know true fear. If I don't do what Scott says, he'll hurt my uncle. He may kill us both.

"Scott, please." I resort to begging. Anything to get Scott away from my uncle. "I'm sorry."

"Damn straight, you'll be sorry."

"I'll go." Tears streak down my cheeks. "I promise. I'll go." I sag in his grip, surrendering to my fate. "Please. Let's go. I'll go with you." My attention shifts from Scott's thunderous gaze to the hall leading back to my uncle's room. "I promise."

Closing my eyes, I silently beg for my uncle to please, please, please, be too weak to get out of bed.

"As soon as we get home, you're going to regret this." He releases my arm and grabs the buckle of his pants, letting me know exactly how my punishment will start.

Spots of black fill my vision. I squeeze my eyes and gasp for breath. The fist around my throat does not lift up. Scott's got a choke-hold on me, and he's not letting up.

"Please ..." I gulp for air. "I can't breathe."

"Who the fuck is that guy? The one you couldn't keep your hands off?"

"Scott ..." My eyes tear. "I c-can't b-breathe."

Scott's body shifts. Pain rips through me, stealing my breath as Scott punches me in the stomach. He follows with a second. And then a third.

"Who. Is. He?" Each word comes with another punch to my gut.

Blinding pain becomes my universe.

Scott pins me to the door. Hand at my throat, he punches hard. My body lifts each time his fist connects.

My vision turns black. My body jerks as each punch hits home. Caught between his fist and the door, my body absorbs all the terrible power fueled by Scott's jealous rage.

A loud crash sounds in the kitchen. I slip in and out of conscious-ness. There's a large shape. Moving fast.

Toward me.

The punches to my gut stop.

Agony rips through me.

Scott's nails scrape my skin as his fingers are ripped from my throat. No longer supported, I slump to the floor. Gasping and gulping, I try to escape. Too weak to stand, I make it to my hands and knees. I crawl, even knowing I won't get far.

Another crash. This one directly over my head.

"Oof!" Scott gasps. He trips over me, stumbling backward, but then his weight suddenly lifts. Scott cries out.

"Abby!" That's my uncle. "What's going on?"

I crawl toward the sound of his voice while a fistfight rages around me. By the time I make it to my uncle, I can see again.

And what I see is death incarnate.

Drake goes toe-to-toe with Scott. Fists fly as the men battle it out. My uncle leans against the wall, wheezing from the exertion of walking less than twenty feet.

Drake's a thing of beauty when he fights. All sinuous grace, he moves with single-minded determination.

His objective is clear.

Eliminate the threat.

Scott's head whips to the left as Drake punches him in the jaw. Blood and spittle fly in an arc. Before Scott recovers, Drake's on him again. This time, with a flurry of punches to Scott's midsection, ending with an uppercut to his jaw. His head whips back.

Drake doesn't stop. He's a trained killing machine, and he's going to kill Scott.

I struggle to my feet and clutch my uncle's hand.

"Go back to your room. Call the cops." We need 9-1-1 before this becomes a homicide.

While my uncle retreats to his room, I gather myself together. With a shake of my head, I clear my vision and steady my feet beneath me.

Scott's body bends beneath the force of Drake's punches. He's already lost, no longer fighting back.

"Drake ..." Barely over a whisper, I can barely hear my own voice.

I rub at the tenderness of my throat and try to ease some of the tightness.

As I swallow, one of Drake's punches sends Scott flying over the back of the sofa. I rush Drake.

My hand goes to his arm, and I flinch as his body tenses.

"The cops are on the way." I tug his arm.

I can only hope Drake understands what I'm trying to say because there's no doubt in my mind, he'll kill Scott.

All the tension in his body suddenly melts. He slings an arm over my shoulder and kisses the crown of my head.

"Are you okay?" His deep voice runs through me, fortifying and lending me strength.

"I'm okay." I'm totally not okay. My entire body shakes with fine tremors as adrenaline rushes through me.

Drake's voice suddenly hardens. "Get up off that sofa and it's the last thing you'll ever do."

I peek over the couch. Fear fills Scott's expression. It vibrates in every molecule of his body. He collapses back on the cushions, heaving and out of breath.

His face is a bloodied mess. His lip's split. One eye is already swollen closed. The other isn't too far behind. Abrasions and bruising along his jaw tell a terrible story.

I grip Drake's bicep with my shaky hand, then run my hand down his arm until our fingers clasp together.

"You saved me." I lean my head against him as we both look down at Scott. "How did you know?"

"When I was leaving, I checked your Jeep. All four tires were slashed. I have a feeling this asshole's been stalking you. No doubt he's behind all of it."

A shiver worms its way down my spine. If that's the case, Scott's been here for well over a week—watching me.

Stalking me.

Bright, blue and red lights flash through the window. Sirens sound a few seconds later. I release Drake and open the door. Two cop cars pull up outside. Down the street, a red and white ambulance follows.

The cops come to the door, take one look at me and draw their guns. The moment they see Drake, the guns go down.

"What's going on?" The question isn't directed to me, but rather to Drake.

27

BOSTON

"Hey, Mitch." Drake knows the cop. "Just taking care of an unwanted guest." Drake points at me. "He assaulted Abby and has been stalking her for well over a week. The bastard likes to hit women. Thinks it makes him a bigger man." Drake turns his stony gaze to Scott, who cowers on my couch. "You're a fucking putz. A tiny man. You're going to get up close and personal with what happens to men who hit women in jail."

Drake takes a step back while Mitch and his partner collect Scott. They haul him up and off my couch, spin him around, and unceremoniously cuff him.

I expect Scott to get in the last word, blaming me like he's done every other time. Instead, he leaves my house, head bowed, shoulders slumped in defeat.

Tom Jenkins and Fred Cavanaugh, my EMTs, wait for the cops to leave with Scott in tow. They exchange words with Mitch, who gives a shake of his head. I guess Scott's going to jail without his injuries tended.

"Doc ..." Fred's jaw drops when he sees me.

Tom follows suit. They rush toward me, pause to let Drake give them room, then fuss over me and my injuries. Their expressions worry me.

"Do I look that bad?"

"Have you looked in a mirror?" Fred puts his medical bag down on the coffee table.

"No."

"Don't." Tom gently grips my chin. He shines a light in my eyes and begins his assessment.

"I'm fine." I bat him away, feeling self-conscious.

"Doc ..." Tom's tone turns serious. "I think you should come with us."

"Why?"

He gestures to his throat. "That bruising concerns me. You need to be observed overnight."

I feel my throat. It's tender and bruised. Swelling. I swallow and note a lump in my throat.

"Where else are you hurt?" Fred places a blood pressure cuff around my arm and guides me to a seat.

I pull up my shirt. All three men wince. No, make that four.

My uncle wobbles into view, looking pale, emaciated, and enraged.

"This is what he's done to you?" The shock of his expression makes him look paler than before.

I give a clipped nod, feeling self-conscious that my private life is no longer private. Give it a few days and everyone in town will know. Not the best way to make an impression.

"Abby, I agree." Uncle Pete examines me. "The bruising on your neck needs to be watched. If it closes off your airway ..."

"I know." I roll my eyes and try to smile.

The scariest thing about this is that I took care of a man when I was a resident. Like me, he was in a fistfight. He was choked. Two hours later, we inserted a breathing tube because the swelling nearly closed his airway off completely.

"I also want to scan your abdomen." My uncle is in doctor mode, triaging my injuries. "Let's get her loaded up."

Before I can protest, Drake comes over. He gathers me in his arms and carries me to the ambulance and waiting gurney. He places me down as gently as he can and brushes the hair out of my eyes.

"I'm going to follow them." He glances over his shoulder. "And help your uncle."

I get what he's saying. My uncle's too weak to make it on his own.

"Thank you." I grip his arm, communicating more in a look than I could in a lifetime of words.

"I'll see you later, city girl." He shakes his head and cracks a smile. "You sure know how to make things interesting."

"I try." My smile is weak and getting weaker by the minute. Fred and Tom load me into the back of the ambulance while I drift in and out of consciousness.

28

RING

OVER THE NEXT WEEK, I SLOWLY HEAL FROM MY INJURIES. MY NECK swelled up, but not enough to close off my airway. I spent the first night under observation in intensive care. Two days on the step-down unit while they scanned and rescanned my abdomen. Initial concerns about a ruptured spleen didn't pan out—thankfully. By day four, I went to the general medicine ward while neurologists watched me, and I regained my strength.

At the one-week mark, they release me.

And Drake is there to take me home.

He hasn't left my side, sitting by me during the entire ordeal.

During the week I'm in the hospital, my uncle's health sharply declines.

* * *

I SIT WITH HIM IN HIS BEDROOM, HOLDING HIS HAND AS HE TAKES HIS last breath. It seems as if half the town has stopped by. The news of his imminent death brought everyone by to say their final goodbyes.

Sara manages the visitors, ushering them out when the end draws near. The entire office staff is present, as are Drake and Bert. Under

Sara's watchful eye, they each say their final goodbyes and leave me to sit by his side.

Despite his struggle to breathe, a smile curls the corners of his mouth. Uncle Pete takes one last breath, then leaves me with peace in his heart. A dignified death speeds his journey to rejoin the love of his life in Heaven.

Tears fall as I leave his room and join Drake. Everyone else is gone. He holds my hand, then holds me as I cry. I don't have to worry about anything. Between Drake and the Hospice Care worker, the necessary calls are made.

Drake stands by my side as the mortuary service comes and goes. He stays with me that night, refusing to leave me alone. We watch our favorite movie, holding hands, sitting side by side.

Words scroll across the screen as the rebels prepare to fight an empire.

At some point, I fall asleep. I don't remember Drake carrying me to bed, but I wake to the most amazing scent floating in the air.

It reminds me of my first day in Peace Springs. I woke to Drake and Bert cooking breakfast for a stranger. Like I did that morning, I follow the delicious scent of bacon in the air. Drake's in the kitchen, cooking for me.

"I love that smell." I sit down at the kitchen table and draw my legs up, knees to chest.

"I thought you would. Bacon and pancakes."

"Mmm, my favorite."

"I know." A mischievous smile lights his face.

I don't know what he's up to, but he's definitely up to something.

Drake places crispy bacon on the table, then two plates with chocolate chip pancakes. My eyes grow wide, as those are my favorite, and I dig in. He takes something from the counter, then joins me at the table. As I shovel bacon into my mouth, he places a sorry-looking plant between us.

Boston's fronds are curled and black. He's had it hard, but I peer into the very center where something sparkles inside.

A diamond glitters with a thousand rainbows.

"Drake ..." My hand goes to my throat as a lump suddenly forms. Tears well in my eyes, but these are happy tears.

Drake lifts the ring from the center of Boston's brutalized foliage and goes to one knee.

"City girl, you are an unexpected treasure. I can't imagine my life without you. I believe fate brought me to you. Since the night I found you struggling on the road, facing down wolves, I've known you were the one. You're the one I want by my side, forever and always. Will you be my wife?"

The tears fall and I can barely see, but I stick my hand out, wiggling my fingers until he slides the ring in place. I cup my hand, staring at the ring. Then I suddenly realize what he did.

"How did you know?"

My attention shifts from the ring on my finger to the tiny shoots of green growing in the very center of Boston. They're tight curls of what will soon be new fronds.

Boston will survive.

I will too.

There's so much I want to do, and for the first time, in a very long time, I can live without fear. I understand better what it means to live in Peace Springs.

In this town, we take care of our own. I thought I would feel incredibly lonely after my uncle passed. Instead, I'm surrounded by friends who care about me and a man who's desperately in love with me.

I've found more than peace. I've found love. I've found friends. I've returned to the place where I most belong.

I've finally found home.

* * *

If you enjoyed Drake and Abby's story, you'll enjoy the other books in The One I Want series, filled with love at first sight, fierce women, and protective ex-military men.

CHECK OUT other books in The One I Want series. CLICK HERE.

Want to keep in touch? Sign up for my Newsletter: elliemasters. com/Newslettersignup and receive a FREE copy of Rescuing Melissa, book 1 in my romantic suspense bestselling series: Guardian Hostage Rescue Specialists.

ELLZ BELLZ
ELLIE'S FACEBOOK READER GROUP

If you are interested in joining the ELLZ BELLZ, Ellie's Facebook reader group, we'd love to have you.

Join Ellie's ELLZ BELLZ.
The ELLZ BELLZ Facebook Reader Group

Sign up for Ellie's Newsletter.
Elliemasters.com/newslettersignup

ALSO BY ELLIE MASTERS

The LIGHTER SIDE

Ellie Masters is the lighter side of the Jet & Ellie Masters writing duo! You will find Contemporary Romance, Military Romance, Romantic Suspense, Billionaire Romance, and Rock Star Romance in Ellie's Works.

YOU CAN FIND ELLIE'S BOOKS HERE:

ELLIEMASTERS.COM/BOOKS

Military Romance

Guardian Hostage Rescue Specialists

Rescuing Melissa

(Get a FREE copy of Rescuing Melissa

when you join Ellie's Newsletter)

Alpha Team

Rescuing Zoe

Rescuing Moira

Rescuing Eve

Rescuing Lily

Rescuing Jinx

Rescuing Maria

Bravo Team

Rescuing Angie

Rescuing Isabelle

Rescuing Carmen

Military Romance

Guardian Personal Protection Specialists

Sybil's Protector

Lyra's Protector

The One I Want Series

(Small Town, Military Heroes)

By Jet & Ellie Masters

EACH BOOK IN THIS SERIES CAN BE READ AS A STANDALONE AND IS ABOUT A DIFFERENT COUPLE WITH AN HEA.

Saving Ariel

Saving Brie

Saving Cate

Saving Dani

Saving Jen

Saving Abby

Rockstar Romance

The Angel Fire Rock Romance Series

EACH BOOK IN THIS SERIES CAN BE READ AS A STANDALONE AND IS ABOUT A DIFFERENT COUPLE WITH AN HEA. IT IS RECOMMENDED THEY ARE READ IN ORDER.

Ashes to New (prequel)

Heart's Insanity (book 1)

Heart's Desire (book 2)

Heart's Collide (book 3)

Hearts Divided (book 4)

Hearts Entwined (book5)

Forest's FALL (book 6)

Hearts The Last Beat (book7)

Contemporary Romance

Firestorm

(KRISTY BROMBERG'S EVERYDAY HEROES WORLD)

Billionaire Romance

Billionaire Boys Club

Hawke

Richard

Brody

Contemporary Romance

Cocky Captain

(VI KEELAND & PENELOPE WARD'S COCKY HERO WORLD)

Romantic Suspense

EACH BOOK IS A STANDALONE NOVEL.

The Starling

~AND~

Science Fiction

Ellie Masters writing as L.A. Warren
Vendel Rising: a Science Fiction Serialized Novel

ABOUT THE AUTHOR

ELLIE MASTERS is a multi-genre and Amazon Top 100 best-selling author, writing the stories she loves to read. These are dark erotic tales. Or maybe, sweet contemporary stories. How about a romantic thriller to whet your appetite? Ellie writes it all. Want to read passionate poems and sensual secrets? She does that, too. Dip into the eclectic mind of Ellie Masters, spend time exploring the sensual realm where she breathes life into her characters and brings them from her mind to the page and into the heart of her readers every day.

Ellie Masters has been exploring the worlds of romance, dark erotica, science fiction, and fantasy by writing the stories she wants to read. When not writing, Ellie can be found outside, where her passion for all things outdoor reigns supreme: off-roading, riding ATVs, scuba diving, hiking, and breathing fresh air are top on her list.

She has lived all over the United States—east, west, north, south and central—but grew up under the Hawaiian sun. She's also been privileged to have lived overseas, experiencing other cultures and making lifelong friends. Now, Ellie is proud to call herself a Southern transplant, learning to say y'all and "bless her heart" with the best of them. She lives with her beloved husband, two children who refuse to flee the nest, and four fur-babies; three cats who rule the household, and a dog who wants nothing other than for the cats to be his best friends. The cats have a different opinion regarding this matter.

Ellie's favorite way to spend an evening is curled up on a couch, laptop in place, watching a fire, drinking a good wine, and bringing forth all the characters from her mind to the page and hopefully into the hearts of her readers.

FOR MORE INFORMATION
elliemasters.com

f facebook.com/elliemastersromance

🐦 twitter.com/Ellie__Masters

📷 instagram.com/ellie_masters

BB bookbub.com/authors/ellie-masters

g goodreads.com/Ellie_Masters

CONNECT WITH ELLIE MASTERS

Website:
elliemasters.com
Amazon Author Page:
elliemasters.com/amazon
Facebook:
elliemasters.com/Facebook
Goodreads:
elliemasters.com/Goodreads
Instagram:
elliemasters.com/Instagram

FINAL THOUGHTS

I hope you enjoyed this book as much as I enjoyed writing it. If you enjoyed reading this story, please consider leaving a review on Amazon and Goodreads, and please let other people know. A sentence is all it takes. Friend recommendations are the strongest catalyst for readers' purchase decisions! And I'd love to be able to continue bringing the characters and stories from My-Mind-to-the-Page.

Second, call or e-mail a friend and tell them about this book. If you really want them to read it, gift it to them. If you prefer digital friends, please use the "Recommend" feature of Goodreads to spread the word.

Or visit my blog https://elliemasters.com, where you can find out more about my writing process and personal life.

Come visit The EDGE: Dark Discussions where we'll have a chance to talk about my works, their creation, and maybe what the future has in store for my writing.

Facebook Reader Group: Ellz Bellz

Thank you so much for your support!

Love,

Ellie

DEDICATION

This book is dedicated to you, my reader. Thank you for spending a few hours of your time with me. I wouldn't be able to write without you to cheer me on. Your wonderful words, your support, and your willingness to join me on this journey is a gift beyond measure.

Whether this is the first book of mine you've read, or if you've been with me since the very beginning, thank you for believing in me as I bring these characters 'from my mind to the page and into your hearts.'

Love,
Ellie

THE END

* * *